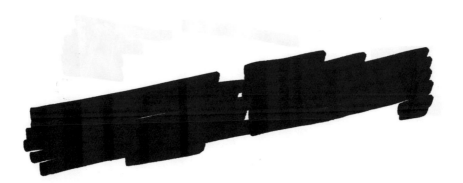

Arena Theatre

Arena Theatre

Dimensions for the Space Age

by

Edwin M. Grove

The Whitston Publishing Company
Troy, New York
1989

Library of Congress Catalog Card Number 87-50838

ISBN 0-87875-344-3

Printed in the United States of America

ACKNOWLEDGEMENTS

The author wishes to offer his sincerest thanks to the following people and organizations who have provided assistance and contributed materials for this book:

Mr. Thomas A. Blount, Blount/Pitman and Associates, Atlanta, GA.

From *Body Language* by Julius Fast. Copyright © 1970 by Julius Fast. Reprinted by permission of the publisher, M. Evans and Company, Inc., 216 E. 49th Street, New York, NY 10017.

California State University, Long Beach, Department of Theater Arts, Mr. Jeff Hickman, Photo Archivist.

Dr. Mal Davidson, Department of Theater, Loyola-Marymount University, Los Angeles, CA.

Mr. Leo Freedman, Beverly Hills, CA.

Miss Elizabeth Ives, Derry, NH.

Kalamazoo Civic Players; James Carver, Managing Director; David Grapes II, Associate Director; Kalamazoo, MI.

Mr. Mezrop Kesdekian, Southern Methodist University, Dallas, TX.

Susanne K. Langer, excerpted from *Feeling And Form.* Copyright © 1953 Charles Scribner's Sons; copyright renewed © 1981 Susanne K. Langer. Reprinted with the permission of Charles Scribner's Sons.

Old Globe Theatre, Simon Edison Center for the Performing

Arts, Cassius Carter Center Stage; San Diego, CA; William Eaton, Public Relations Director.

Mr. Vincent Piacintini, St. Louis, MO.

Dr. Jerry Pickering, Department of Theater Arts, California State University, Fullerton.

Theatre Three, Dallas, TX; Norma Young, Founding/Artistic Director; Jack Alder, Executive Producer-Director; Gary Yawn, Administrative/Public Relations.

Mrs. Betty Rice Trott, Columbus, OH.

Tufts University, Theater Department, Medford, MA.

Mr. Robert Wolff, ARTEC Consultants, New York, NY.

Mr. Kelly Yeaton, Professor Emeritus, Pennsylvania State University, Department of Theatre Arts.

LIST OF ILLUSTRATIONS

LIST OF FIGURES

CONTENTS

SPECIFYING THE CASE FOR ARENA THEATRE

FOREWORD

The modern American theatre in all its many manifestations and diverse methods of staging has often carried the boundaries of experimentation in production methods well beyond the normal expectations of any playwright's drama. Various techniques of production have been applied, sometimes with profoundly artistic results, to old plays that were thought to be more or less empty of further potential for illumination. At the same time, some scripts have been utterly ruined by production experiments and unique staging methods. In something more than a manner of speaking, there are no rules for production in the American theatre; generally, anything the theatre artist wants to try goes, and the results can often be as chaotic as they are iconoclastic.

Among the various methods that have become more or less standardized from theatre company to theatre company, however, certain staging techniques have emerged as being the most popular. Quite obviously, the traditional proscenium method using a main drape and box set (or not) remains at the forefront of most companies' repertoire, but in the course of the past four decades in particular, the evolution of a number of other types of stages—thrust, three-quarter-round, two-sided stages, etc.—have also emerged. Some of these have been born of necessity, as not all companies, amateur or even professional, have the funds required to construct a traditional theatre and must operate in buildings singularly ill-suited for theatrical production. But acting on the presumption that the design of a theatre's stage is to some degree deliberate and the result of thoughtful formatting and planning by a company's managers and directors, the question must be raised as to the logic behind the design of any stage for any singular purpose. It must never be left to chance, and it must accommodate both the medium and the message of the plays the company plans to produce.

"Theatre-in-the-round" or arena staging was for a short time about thirty years ago, very popular. Early experiments in this production form were more than somewhat successful, but for one reason or another, they have lost popularity in recent years. Certainly economics plays a part in the declining enthusiasm for arena staging, for clearly, a company can seat more people in a proscenium setting than it can in the traditional "little theatre" concept of arena. Arena staging also poses logistical problems for productions with regard to lighting, costuming, properties, handling, etc., which are more easily overcome in other forms. Even so, the mistake that so many theatre artists have made over the years has been to regard arena staging as simply an alternative method to proscenium or other staging devices. The purpose of this text is to advance the notion that arena is not only a unique and artistically sound method of staging many plays, but that it also is a virtual metaphor for a modern age, an age that has put increasing importance on the notion of space.

Heretofore, theatrical manuals concerned with arena staging have confined themselves to dealing with the "How" of arena productions, with methods of overcoming logistical difficulties in actual productions and suggesting acting and directing approaches that are unique to the round form. None, however, has addressed the question of "Why?" The result has been a decline in interest in arena staging at the very time when such a production method seems to be most appropriate. But one needs only to view productions in today's arena theatres to understand why there is little clamor to create any longer in a round medium. The essence of the problem is that many theatre artists tend to view arena as merely another means to a production's end, not as a part of the entire artistic performance that has a direct bearing on a play's presentation and is integrally a part of the aesthetic and rhetorical whole.

This book, therefore, undertakes to discuss the question of "Why Arena Theatre?" The surface concerns of charm and charisma must quickly be penetrated to arrive at a deeper meaning behind the creative process involved in staging plays in a round format. Arena has an aesthetic singularity all its own; and through it, arena is pertinent to special psycho-socio-political and ethologic implications that are implicit in the round form. The proper understanding of why arena staging is more than merely a theatrical method can lead to the creation of fine works of art that mesh form and content for a more complete artistic whole.

Working theatre artists might object to an intellectual approach to a fundamental staging method. Their objections would likely stem from the idea that the staging of a play belongs to a set of pragmatic questions having nothing to do with the art they would want to create. Such an attitude has led, I believe, to the disarray of contemporary

American theatre and to a confusing approach to staging methods.

Drama is very likely the oldest of the lively arts. Even dance and music could be theorized as having developed to accompany primitive story telling in mime form among pre-lingual societies. Regardless, for the past twenty-five hundred years, people's love of theatre and dedication to it as an experience that permits them to intuitively and vicariously examine their own lives is well documented. Since Aristotle, the public devotion to theatre and the dramas staged therein has been a fundamental part of civilization. Further, among all the arts, the theatre is the most constantly changing and developing form; its innovations and trial and error of new methods respond almost directly to the needs of those who come to see it.

The same public which is devoted to theatre and its innovations, however, also shuns exploitation. Audiences are hard to fool, and the presentation of poorly conceived productions usually is met by deliberate ignorance and ultimate failure. The theatre company which stubbornly clings to traditional methods is likely soon to be regarded as static, mundane, boring. Conversely, the theatre company which uses innovative forms—particularly arena staging—but uses it improperly or does not select plays which are conducive to the method, risks being accused of confusion, short-sightedness, and poor artistic conceptualization. The modern theatre, beset as it is with competition from other media, finds itself required to present deliberate purpose and to excite artistic sensibilities in order to captivate its audiences and provide them with the fulfillment they have come to expect from the dramatic form.

Arena staging is very likely the theatrical method best suited to satisfy this requirement, for arena staging is the best form to assist modern man in understanding his human condition. However, it is necessary for those who would use arena as a vehicle for their productions to have a full awareness of the connotative and sometimes subliminal effects of staging plays in the round. They must understand that arena is not merely an alternative method to staging but that it contains within it nuances and suggestions that tend to shape—or perhaps reshape—the very meaning of the plays produced in round space. The rewards of such understanding can be great, but the penalties for misapplying the form or for misunderstanding its significance to modern theatre are equally large.

Possibly, arena staging might be regarded as the most important theatrical form for this age that concentrates so much on the concept of space in all its manifestations; if this is true, then it follows that theatre, our oldest and most significant "mirror" of life, should utilize space with the same modern eye in order to draw the maximum effect from the drama of human existence.

INTRODUCTION

Almost anyone who has even a nodding acquaintance with the modern theatre likely has seen an amateur or collegiate production of a play staged "in-the-round." So-called "studio theatres" have provided the opportunity for various experiments in theatrical forms for years, particularly on college campuses. The development of "thrust," "three-quarter-round," "two-sided-round," and other methods of staging productions have been born out of the imaginations of theatre managers and academic directors, and some have achieved a sufficient degree of popularity to be copied and established as permanent staging constructs for little theatre groups across the country. Further, the popularity of "dinner theatres" during the sixties and seventies stretched the resources of staging ideas about as far as they could be. In one dinner theatre in Tulsa, Oklahoma, for example, patrons were seated in an ordinary restaurant's format, and the play, when it began, worked its way around tables and waiters' aisles and utilized a patch of hard-wood flooring that doubled as a dancing area for private parties. In a production of *See Saw* in the mid-seventies, the jukebox was covered with painted cardboard and was treated as a bureau.

Other amateur and little theatre notions—some born of economic necessity—flourish coast to coast, and "in-the-round" productions are quite common. But fewer patrons of the professional stage than might be imagined have experienced arena productions, and an astonishing number of theatre professionals have never worked on any arena stage at all.

During auditions for an arena production of an Equity-waiver production of *One Flew Over the Cuckoo's Nest* in Los Angeles last year, only one Equity actor out of twenty or so had any previous arena experience at all. When one considers how few actors find work in the legitimate theatre, this might not be surprising; however, what it reveals mostly is how "short-changed" actors have been in terms of their theatre experience. The twenty-some-odd actors who had no arena experience in their backgrounds were deficit at one of the best crucibles for refining their skills because they lacked this vitally important training. Yet even more profoundly indicting than the absence of such mechanical experience among actors is the deprivation of the public by the failure of professional companies to use a true arena format. Such a widespread dearth of arena productions impoverishes our national theatre, trivializes much of the remaining art of contemporary drama, and inhibits the continuing maturation and importance of the dramatic form as a mirror of mankind's social character.

Those are rather heavy responsibilities to impute to arena theatres, perhaps. What is an arena theatre, after all, to justify this sort of assertion? Isn't an arena stage merely a method of production which brings the play into the middle of the playhouse and surrounds it with an audience? Actually, it is much more than that. The location of the stage and audience does not define arena theatre. Such a definition is little more than a description of how an arena theatre is configured and fails to do more than evoke much more than an elementary notion of what happens in an arena production or, more importantly, what is *supposed to happen* there.

A description, then, is only a beginning of a discussion of the importance of understanding the entire concept and dramaturgical philosophy behind arena staging; but it is a beginning, and by way of introducing the concept of arena staging, it is important to understand the differences between arena staging and other innovations of the modern stage. By viewing photographs of specific arena productions, it might be possible to augment the description and start to approach the deeper implications in this particular staging method. The following photographs were taken at various theatres and provide a series of glimpses that suggest a two-dimensional notion of the effects of arena staging. Although the limits of photography are self-evident, these views provide a starting place for a deeper investigation of the impact of arena theatre on modern drama.

Model, Arena Stage in Washington, DC, with roof raised

Interior of Le Théâtre en Rond de Paris.
This theatre has seating for 300.

"Dr. Faustus Lights The Lights," California State University, Long Beach, 1981

"Guys and Dolls," by Loesser, Wurzburg, West Germany

"The Venetian Twins," 1971-2, Theatre Three, Dallas, Texas

"Love's Comedy," by Henrik Ibsen, Tufts Arena Theatre

Interior, Cassius Carter Centre Stage, San Diego, California

"The Boys in the Band," Kalamazoo [Michigan] Civic Players

"You Can't Take It With You," California State University, Long Beach, 1980

Lobby, The Octagon Theatre, [Montgomery] Alabama Shakespeare Festival

Interior, The Octagon Theatre, [Montgomery] Alabama Shakespeare Festival

"Streamers"
Kalamazoo [Michigan] Civic Players

AN HISTORICAL OVERVIEW

As the last decade of the twentieth century opens, there no longer remains much academic dispute over the historical evolution of arena theatre. A number of texts, in whole or in part, have sorted through evidence that traces arena's roots back to the earliest beginnings of theatre. Twenty-five years ago such preponderant agreement as to where arena theatre actually began could not have been supposed. Regardless of whether one attributed arena to ancient antecedents or saw it strictly as a modern invention, such views tended to color one's assessment of the essential character of arena theatre. Unfortunately, during those days one encountered more anxiety for connecting various styles of playwriting to arena staging than for finding the philosophical impact of making the theatre itself round. Theoretically, the result of such investigation seemed much like forcing the square peg into the round hole.

By the 1980's, all the clamor that arena was meant to be the spearhead for this or that dramaturgical mode seems to have faded. In certain respects, today's less emotional atmosphere is healthier for a normal maturation of valid arena practice and theory. By now, other forms of theatre no longer feel threatened. On the other hand, missing nowadays is the portentous excitement and frenetic zeal which once moved arena proponents in earlier days. The revolution which was once trumpeted for theatre-in-the-round has simply never materialized, at least with anything resembling first expectations. Throughout the United States and the world there are a number of fully professional arena theatres, to be sure. Notable among them is the Arena Stage in Washington, D.C., which resides in a fine multi-million dollar edifice built to its precise specifications. Yet such an institution no longer ranks among the avant-garde; it has become an institution of the conservative and respectable theatre establishment. And faded by that distinction is its power to alter forever the face of theatre.

Although the general theatre-going public is often less concerned with the method of staging a play than with the quality of the production or script, the unique, aesthetic character of arena staging in the modern theatre has such an important impact on a play and its interpretation, that a full understanding of its implications is necessary. Unlike numerous other theatrical techniques, arena theatre is not merely a culmination of certain direct historical trends or paths. To suggest that it is nothing more than an outgrowth of a logical progression of theatrical development serves only to apologize for the form and to suggest that it, like numerous fads and experiments of the theatre, is a passing fancy, something that offers little more than scintillating and momentary illumination and will fade as new ideas are advanced. In short, to view arena theatre as being simply a part of theatre history is too limiting. Even so, a survey of the history of dramatic forms can lead to the threshold of arena theatre. After that, however, a new code of conduct for staging plays must be observed. The old parameters are no longer adequate to explain the prevailing conditions.

A. Currents that merged in the early theatrical experience

Dramatic art is traditionally considered to have emerged out of Stone-Age tribal rituals and magic. Since little actual evidence survives, scholars commonly surmise that drama and mimesis are each by-products of the dance art, which, in its infancy, was based upon religious negotiation. Harvest and fertility rites were the actual circumstances from which the early Greek dramatic presentations sprang; but the impetus for religious worship, dance performance, and the dramatic arts each seemed to originate from the same spiritual font. This accounts for the awed sense of reverence maintained by the Greeks for all theatre. Its broad ethical overtones effected for them the "holy office" of propitiating sensitive or capricious Gods.

Tribal societies through all parts of the world have similarly seemed to employ the dance as a mode of negotiation with unseen powers, the spirits and Gods. This form of expression persists up to the present day, and seems as intrinsic to human nature as speech, which it even precedes.[1]

The dance began its history with movements that were probably reflective of commonplace activities in the life of primitive man: hunting, stalking of prey, discovery of shelter, mating, the birth of children, victory in battle, etc. Initially dance movement was purely utilitarian as the tribes gathered around in a circle to witness actual happenings; these gradually evolved into storytelling events with dramatic action. In time they were imbued with all the importance of rituals. As such rituals became formalized and traditional among tribes and, ultimately, civilizations, they were taught and handed down from generation to generation, and each successive group of performers likely added their own innovations and techniques as their abilities and imaginations permitted.

Learning a hunting or mating dance served the dual purpose of teaching the young how the process is done and of passing along a method of that teaching which often became as important to the process as the subject of the ritual itself. Thus, the entire notion of man's survival expanded as a concept that encompassed both the necessary activities of life and the accompanying instructional ritual as well. As time passed and civilization became more formalized, such rituals often became religious in their overtones, and sometimes the spiritual meaning of the ritualized movement and performance might have been forgotten in the intricacies of the preserved form. For example, one might theorize that the indispensable factor of the actual hunt became less important to the ritual than the need for the spiritual magic of the ritual to guarantee that the hunt would be successful.

With the addition of the idea of sacrifice as a measure of guarantee or appeasement, the primitive religious, mythic conscious-ness was complete. A process that was purely utilitarian in inception became spiritually essential as it was refined and perfected through generations of preservation and enhancement. Dance became, in short, an abstract interaction with incomprehensible forces outside the human beings who performed it.

One of the earliest forms of such primitive dance, the "chain dance" was specifically designed to fulfill a "holy office," and it was understood to be quite different from mere spontaneous prancing in emotional reaction to unexpected developments in life. Man's devel-opment from hunter and gatherer to cultivator and keeper of domestic beasts brought new significance to the seasons for planting and harvest. Such dance rituals called *Reigen*, the "circle dances," are noteworthy not only for the significance of their close relationship to primitive nature religion but also because of their circular form.

The circular form of the *Reigen* was accidental, at least in part; it probably sprang from the necessary encirclement to catch a prey. But it also was deliberate in the sense that, although the dance motive was not yet a formal performance for any sort of audience, it was intended to be a negotiation of power with unseen forces. André

Villiers has observed that the rhythmic beat inherent to such dances would virtually compel the dancers, in an obvious sense, to conform to the span of a circle, rather than the wandering off into tangential lines.[3] And Arnold Haskell in *The Wonderful World of Dance* states the "Farandole" is such a chain dance on the motif of "going and returning to the heart of the labyrinth."[4]

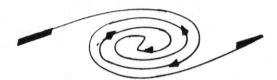

Figure 1
Pattern of a Farandole

Certainly, primitive dance had only "ecstatic" purpose, a sharing by the dancer in the feeling of power. If there were any spectators whatsoever, they most likely surrounded the dancers informally. But informally or not, the operative word here is *surrounded*, for in these ritual movements of early man, most likely, were experienced the initial, primitive spontaneous elements of an *arena situation*. Little by little, the dance's personages' roles were relegated to the best negotiators of power—a shaman, witch doctor, spiritualist, holy man, wizard, magician, priest, etc. These became surrogates for the tribe, and, at last, the tribe's members assumed the function of audience and vicarious participant rather than performer.

As the dances became more and more formalized and masks, disguises, costumes, phalluses, and other props were added to enhance the ritual and facilitate the negotiation, the dance began to take on story content. Such stories eventually were used to project upon the spectators cures, purifications, initiations, and ultimately recalled heroic deeds, legends, and histories of emerging societies. With the introduction of music and spoken language, the birth of the dramatic arts might be marked. Although still deeply infused with religious meaning and ritualistic behavior, there is little doubt among scholars that drama found its origins in such primitive dance performances.

At that watershed moment of primitive theatrical history, two possible evolutionary paths of conjecture may be followed to the modern arena theatre. Each reflects directly upon the merits of arena staging, but there is no substantial proof that either point of view is correct. Ultimately, it is a matter of likelihood.

Stephen Joseph's book, *Theatre in the Round*, suggests the following rationale for the architectural emergence of theatre structures:

> The demand for a theatre structure arose naturally out of the popularity of the drama. When a lot of people gathered together to watch a performance, the circle of spectators could see better if those outside were raised above the people in front of them. Sloping ground would help. But it is difficult to find a natural theater for a wholly surrounding audience; most hills only partially surround a convenient acting arena—simple craters are uncommon and usually unsuitable anyhow. So the Greek theaters, while retaining the circular acting areas, nestled against hillsides that provided only a partially surrounding auditorium.[5]

A second version of such an architectural emergence of theatres, however, is equally plausible. The trouble is that it would demonstrate how the round was simply never regarded as conducive to the oratorical performance of *drama*. One could very well argue that the introduction of spoken language to relate stories made it imperative to place focus on the "agonist" (speaking performer) distinct from the circle of dancers, or, eventually, chorus. Eventually these agonists were even situated on a podium in front of a scene-house ("proskene") face to face with the spectators. This version of the events suggests a natural evolvement born of the perceived necessity to fix special spectator attention on the storyteller. According to surviving records, the first drama began with only one actor and the chorus. We know the chorus continued to dance and chant as it had always done, in the circle. But from where was the actor actually speaking his lines?

Both views have merit. To portray dramatic evolution along the lines Stephen Joseph has suggested is to link arena theatre with the earliest form of western theatre, its very foundation-stone. The second view confers greater legitimacy to the argument that arena is an aberrant dramatic form, since even the Greeks were impelled to single the actor out from the circular choric ensemble and make him face his audience. Some constitute this as evidence that arena is ill-suited to the aesthetic requirements of the histrionic arts, at least those based on formal speech to large audiences; and the essence of Greek discussion was the simple discipline for *taking turns* in speech, a formality also basic to the Greek drama.

Joseph's account is certainly more congenial to champions of arena theatre, but it does not entirely satisfy. Among no existing ruins of Greek theatres—early or late—is there evidence of any formal design other than amphitheatre. A casual observation could lead to the easy confusion of arena with the amphitheatre form—the altar, after all, is at the center of the orchestra area and the plays as well as their choral dances evolved around that central circle—but the two forms are actually quite different. Joseph's hypothesis seems more wishful than accurate, for no evidence exists that anything resembling a true arena form was ever used by agonist characters to perform Greek drama. If the arena form were, in fact, the foundation stone of dramatic arts (as distinguished from the dithyrambic dance elements), surely at least one theatre or ruin would exist to bear it out. Joseph's supposition that this was because of a dearth of suitable natural sites lacks credibility as well. Narrow canyons abound in Attic Greece. Such arroyos would have allowed audiences to situate themselves all around if the Greek theatre artists had ever deemed such arrangements to be satisfactory for the recital of agonistic speeches.

Since denying Joseph's view depends upon a defense of arena theatre against detractors on other grounds, however, it seems more prudent to conclude at this point that the Greeks departed from the round form once they actually began agonistic oration. The actor was quite deliberately placed with his back to one side, his face to the audience. Extant ruins and surviving contemporary descriptions support no other view.

Regardless of how one portrays the actual physical dawning of drama, as distinguished from elements of the dance, one cannot discount the character of the events from which it sprang. The circular form of dance, mimesis, and the motive of power negotiation were unquestionable progenitors to the drama. Based on those factors, the ancient *arena impulse*, and everything it implies to the development of modern arena theatre may be more clearly understood.

Obviously, all kinds of situations where arena *could* have been employed for performances have existed throughout dramatic arts history. In truth, very little evidence substantiates such speculation. Even when the probabilities defie, often as not, available facts do not offer convincing proof of the use of arena. Indeed, one must leap all the way from the Greeks to the Middle Ages before encountering sure evidence that performances in-the-round were given.

B. Performance modes of the Mystery plays

Until fairly recent times it was generally assumed that the English Mystery plays were all performed on rolling carts that travelled through city streets. That perception was gathered chiefly from the accounts of one Archdeacon Rogers, who died in the year 1595, and who was thought, perhaps incorrectly, to have witnessed the very last of such performances before the Mystery plays were finally suppressed by the church. The Mystery plays were begun as early as the twelfth century and were originally played inside the churches by the priests themselves. Throughout the nearly four hundred years of their sway, one must assume that much was altered about the manner in which the plays were produced. At the very least they were moved outdoors, and became the handiwork of various trades guilds.

Principally due to the research of Richard Southern, scholars now realize that actors in the Mystery plays actually traversed from one "mansion" stage to another during such performances. This raises a question how actors could manage to do this if such stages were mobile and rolling down streets during a performance which had been supposed to have been viewed intermittently by spectators along the way.[6]

Indeed, a Cornish Mystery play which was overlooked by English and Latin scholars for centuries, has fostered a whole new notion about how such plays were performed. Richard Southern finally translated the text, known as *The Castle of Perseverance*, from the Cornish and found indication that its wagons were drawn up stationary in an arrangement roughly approximating the perimeter of a circle—perhaps in a town plaza or marketplace. Specifically the text refers to such an arrangement in one of the Cornish "Rounds," which were originally ancient potteryworks, but later adapted for athletic events, joustings, fairs, and as is now realized, the performance of plays. In the center of this circle a scaffold structure was erected which was enclosed to represent the "Castle." In the text the actors were given explicit directions to move about from mansion to mansion, as the scenes required. But more pertinently, they also moved to the castle in the center, and played some portion of their scenes in and out of that castle.

Such published evidence shows how at least some minor portions of that particular play were sent into the midst of the spectators. It would be problematic to infer broad aesthetic insights from this example, since the central area evidently serviced basically

as a midpoint between actions carried out on the various wagon
stages. Nonetheless, it demonstrates there was no hesitation about
extending action right out into the midst of audiences. Sensibilities
were not violated when the story enactment was brought into physical
touch with the spectators. No conventional wisdom demanded that
the actors should always need to face the percipients.

To the largely illiterate populace, those plays held great sway.
The people reacted with intense involvement, to a degree which
would be difficult for modern-day spectators to imagine. The Miracle
plays which preceded the Mysteries had been forced out of the
churches and priests forbidden to act in them. The power of involvement became too strong for any who were associated to remain
contemplative. The Church generally held that the charged responses
of the spectators were too-easily diverted to the profane.

Is there an echo of the Greek dramatic experience in these
examples of the Miracle and Mystery Plays? To a limited degree, at
least, there is a similarity insofar as the plays took on the import of a
"holy office." Indeed the passions of the populace were so stirred by
them that the clergy ultimately scorned the plays as dangerous,
impious, and idolatrous.[7] The problem was not in getting audiences
to pay attention to the biblical lessons of the plays; for, unquestionably, the clergy wished to inculcate those lessons. Rather, the audience's close proximity to the action simply caught up and enthralled
too much crowd attention and passion. The psychic threshold of
power negotiation was being approached through such productions;
it bordered upon the sort of "ecstatic" state which is similar, perhaps,
to a frenzy induced by voodoo, or recognized in another guise as the
impassioned mob hysteria. Aside from the form—the mob's appetite
for *entertainment* (lavish display, rough comedy, sensuous figures,
music and fighting) was plainly engulfing an orderly showing of a
Biblical story. Hence the fear arose that such plays were an imminent
threat to ecclesiastical authority. The Church ultimately suppressed
the plays.

C. Points about the Elizabethan theatre structures

The Elizabethan "public" theatres have usually been characterized as open stages—with audiences situated more or less on three
sides of the acting area. Stephen Joseph asserts that this characteriza-

tion may not be entirely true.[8] He claims, for example, that the Globe theatre was used not only for plays, but its inn-yard, and others, were sometimes sites for fencing matches, acrobatics, bear-baiting, and other entertainments. The center of the courtyard was employed for such activities, and the stage platform we commonly presume as the unique feature of "Shakespearean houses" was merely a temporary structure. He goes so far as to add that, on occasion, such platforms were dispensed with, in favor of using the center of the courtyard to perform the plays. He draws a picture for our imagination of "tiring houses" being employed at either end of the building, one end representing "heaven's gate," and the other end "hellmouth," which were concepts carried over from the earlier Mystery plays.

Proof of the hypothetical existence of such arrangements defies solid verification. However, Joseph reprints one curious engraving that can be found on the title page of one of Ben Jonson's folios.[9] Certain letters written in 1616 by Ben Jonson to an engraver, a Mr. William Hole, set down in writing its exact specifications. It was to depict a group of actors in what appears to be a circular performing arena. This unprecedented engraving fosters some astonishing rumination about which model Jonson had in mind when he commissioned the artist to prepare it. Besides the reprints of that engraving and letter, no other information about Elizabethan staging has survived to confirm, one way or another, whether Elizabethan "public" theatre sometimes played shows in-the-round or not.

A more solid foundation exists for citing an arena precedent among the Masques from the accounts of their performances in royal courts and castles. Some drawings left by the great designer, Inigo Jones, and stage direction references in a few of Ben Jonson's texts indicate that some action was occasionally played in the center of the great court halls. Even so, the Masques were chiefly spectacles of remarkable stage machinery. Furthermore, the great discovery of Renaissance art was the geometrical structure of *perspective . . . an illusion for the one-eyed*! Indeed, perspective is built in terms of a single view-point, not a ring of them. As such the ruling concept of the Masques had little concern for any principles of arena theatre. Ultimately they were scenic masterworks, meant to be witnessed for the facade. Inigo Jones' elaborate settings were the scenic forebears of the Italian Proscenium-arch tradition that flourished between 1680 and 1780 at the hands of the notable Bibiena family.[10] In spite of the specimen which the Masques offered of scenes played in the center of a large room, these do not offer any enlightening examples of com-

monly understood aesthetic concepts about arena theatre. Their
aesthetic purpose was linked singularly to scenic investiture.

From the Jacobean era until the latter half of the nineteenth
century one finds almost no prescriptive use of theatre-in-the-round.
Isolated, random instances might be traced of near-Eastern or cham-
ber-theatre performances which one might deduce were centrally
staged. But, overall, no indication exists of a concerted, effective
march toward the conscious use of the round form. If employed at all,
expedience instead of aesthetic insight would be said to have gov-
erned the endeavor.

D. Ferment of the new stagecraft

Paradoxically the major catalyst for the twentieth century
arena movement was, in all likelihood, the Naturalistic fourth-wall
convention used on the proscenium stage. Upon the advent of mid-
nineteenth century realistic drama, the drop-and-wing-type stage
gave way to the box setting. Increasingly greater concern was paid to
authenticity and a semblance of the real, in acting, in stage dialogue,
in subject matter, as *well* as in settings. Thus when the performer
walked to the curtain line—presumed to be the position of the room's
fourth wall—yet continued to gaze and speak out toward the audience, such actions often appeared starkly incongruous and "stagey."
Daring realistic directors like the great reformer, André Antoine,
made actors turn their backs to the audiences.[11] Actors, he believed,
were supposed to depict real human beings in real circumstances. An
actor playing with his back to spectators creates an extraordinary
artistic precedent with complex implications. The significance of such
manipulation lies in what it implies about the essential audience/
actor relationship, and the possible extent to which one can amplify
that relationship.

The seminal theoretician behind the modern arena theatre was
actually Adolph Appia. This Swiss-born designer became an early
Guru of "the new stagecraft" movement about 1895, and it was the
intellectual ferment of that movement which presently spawned the
modern arena idea. Appia was discontented with the expressive
limitations or confinements demanded by the box settings, but he was
even more unwilling to see painters reassert control over the theatre.
His first treatise, *The Staging of Wagnerian Drama*, contained not even

one illustration, so determined was he to adhere to his theory. MacGowan and Melnitz described Appia's approach this way:

> His basic aim was "to strengthen the dramatic action." This was to be done not only through the setting, but quite as much through the lighting. His purpose was not to put on an exciting visual show. He wanted to serve the actor. "It is the presence of the actor upon the stage which causes dramatic action; without actors there would be no action." He did not throw out false perspective merely because it was false. He wanted a "plastic," or three-dimensional, set because the actor had that quality, and because the actor's movement could only have meaning in relation to ob- stacles and "points of support offered it by the ground and by natural objects." This made Appia design settings that had a kind of solid reality, as well as various levels for the actors to work upon.[12]

It was not merely the plasticity of the three-dimensional objects he employed, but also his concept that stage lighting served an organic function beyond mere illumination which made Appia the clear theoretical prophet to those who devised theatre-in-the-round. Appia called for "living light," which would change in conjunction with his three-dimensional settings to express the passage of time and denote the play's action in sharper relief. Appia, describing how he would stage Wagner's opera, *Siegfreid*, claimed, "We should no longer try to create the illusion of a forest, but instead the illusion of a man in the atmosphere of a forest . . . the spectators should see Siegfreid bathed in moving lights and shadows, and not the movement of rags of canvas agitated by stage tricks."[13] Philosophically, Appia was break- ing new ground. The harvest his disciples would finally reap from this soil might have astonished even the master, for it ultimately led to foresaking the two-dimensional stage, with its attempt to create the illusion of space by pictorial means.

Gordon Craig, another key visionary of "new stagecraft," like- wise kindled the imaginations of theatre experimentalists seeking to redefine the experience of dramatic arts. In particular, he advocated employing the stage and its setting as a symbolic expression of the play's idea. He especially railed against the influence of painters in the theatre.[14] He called for a sort of cleansed theatre which would eliminate their contamination.

Beginning in approximately the 1880's, a restless creative tur- moil began in the theatre. Proponents of realism waged a caustic rivalry in print against advocates of various more-"theatricalized" styles, as one camp or the other sought preeminence. Lugné-Poë and Jacques Copeau endeavored to counteract the trendy realism of André Antoine and Otto Brahm. In Russia, Meyerhold revolted against the realism of his early mentors, Stanislavski and Nemirovich-Danchenko. England observed the efforts of William Poel to restore authentic Elizabethan staging gaining little ground toward combating the popularity of J. T. Grein's realistic Independent Theatre. August Strindberg, the Swedish playwright, began his career in the mold of Ibsen, a realistic writer, only to reverse his style in later years when his non-realistic plays much more assumed the tone of Belgian, Maurice Maeterlinck.[15] New modes, new styles, new forms, freedom of artistic imagination, experimentation—such was the mood of the age. Invention, in and out of theatre, was the spirit to be noted everywhere.

Among the confusing thrusts and parrys of divergent artistic trends—pro- or anti-realist—were efforts to ally arena theory to one faction or the other. Both the realist Antoine and the works of theatricalist Copeau advance the arena theory and provide valuable resource information. Both notions argue well a favorable case for arena theatre in spite of the fact that the two men represented antithetical stylistic views. For example, Antoine's treatment of the fourth-wall, wittingly or not, redefined the audience/actor relationship. Copeau, for his part, merely carried that new definition one logical, architectural step beyond Antoine: he banished the proscenium arch and obliterated the distinction between stage house and audience house—fusing the two together. In a strict literal sense neither is philosophically closer to central staging, but from Copeau's architectural structure there is a growing impulse to draw the play toward the audience. Copeau, like Poel and the Elizabethans, brought play and audience back into a shared space, a single hall.

Actually, all these theatre styles, realistic and non-realistic alike, were grappling for pertinent, artistically honest and relevant modes of expression. If art mirrors life, then those artists should all be regarded as having sought satisfactory ways to display their art. A special inspiration to arena theory derives from among the realists' camp in advice from the American stage director, Arthur Hopkins.[16] No less a stimulus, though, can be traced to the plastic, three-dimensional stage-use of two German expressionist directors, Leopold Jessner and Jürgen Fehling. Arena apologists must gratefully accept encouragement in whatever guise it can be found.

A chronological table listing events or works from all camps traces the history of an emergent arena theatre medium. The Saxe-Meiningen company, formed in 1866, revolutionized theatre and

Table I

Central Staging Chronology

Year	Important Activity
1866	Duke of Saxe-Meiningen formed theatre company.
1876	Richard Wagner built Beyreuth Festspielhaus.
1879	Invention of incandescent lamp.
1880	Popularizing of Realism. (Naturalism)
1881	Paris Opera, first theatre to use electric lighting.
1886	William Poel staged *Helen of Troy* at Hengler's Circus.
1887	André Antoine began Théâtre Libre, "humanizing theatre."
1889	Otto Brahm opened Freie Bühne in Berlin.
1895	Adolph Appia published *The Staging of Wagnerian Drama* and *Musical Stage Production*.
1898	Lugné-Poë staged *Measure For Measure* at Cirque d'Ete.
1905	Popularizing "new stagecraft movement."
1905	Edward Gordon Craig published *The Art of the Theater*.
1910	Max Reinhardt began conversion of Circus Schumann into Grosses Schauspielhaus. Opened in 1911. Staged massive neo-Greek spectacles.
1913	Jacques Copeau opened Vieux-Columbier theatre in Paris.
1914	Adzubah Latham staged *arena* production of *Mask of Joy* at Columbia University in New York City.
1914	Alexander Tairov opened Kamerny Theatre in Russia.
1919	Firmen Gémier staged *Oedipus* at Cirque d'Hiver in Paris.
1919	Leopold Jessner began using famous Jessner *treppen* (steps).
1920	Arthur Hopkins directing.
1920	Robert Edmund Jones designed *The Cenci* for arena.
1921	Kenneth Macgowen worked on *The Threatre of Tomorrow* at Cirque Medrano.
1922	Norman Bel Geddes planned "Theatre No. 14" project.
1924	Gilmore Brown established Pasadena Playhouse.
1925	Vsevolod Meyerhold and Eugene Vakhtangov experiment in Moscow.
1932	Glenn Hughes set up original Penthouse Theatre in Seattle.
1932	Okhlopkov set up Realistic Theatre, staged *Mother* in Moscow.
1939	Albert McCleary began *arena* theatre at Fordham University in New York, after earlier experiments at Evanston, Illinois, in 1933-4. Disciple of Gilmore Brown.
1940	New Penthouse Theatre designed and constructed at University of Washington in Seattle.

introduced the independent role of stage director. Their renowned ensemble treatment of crowd-scenes astonished a world that had never conceived of masses of performers being physically molded as agents of expression. Large groups, previously unimagined as a device for dramatic manifestation, were unharnessed, and communicated as eloquently as the spoken word. These innovations initiated the first step of the movement toward a modern arena theatre; from these the path moves forward until the outbreak of World War II.

E. Rationalizing the arena theatre

A rapid increase in interest in arena theatres sprang up around the mid-twentieth century. Those who rushed to the battlements to work in the arena form seemed not altogether sure what they had gotten themselves into, and, indeed, any explanations as to why immediately. The question, "Why arena theatre?" encountered a paucity of solid rationale. The theatre's impulsive love-affair with "the round" earned scoldings from certain academicians and critics. Henry Popkin, Arch Lauterer, John Gassner, and Eric Bentley, among them, questioned the artistic viability of arena productions. One rather virulent rebuke came with this declaration by Charles Marowitz: "One is always hearing that theatre-in-the-round confers a much greater reality . . . as an *a priori* virtue of arena staging this is, of course, bosh."[17] He went on to criticize arena theatre principally because it fails to focus audience attention in the fashion of proscenium theatres. This critical barrage[18] forced a much-needed sense of introspection upon proceedings of the arena movement. It fostered an effort to supply an artistic *raison d'etre* among students and proponents of arena staging.

Four chief schools of thought offer a "cause" for the existence of arena theatres up to the present date; that is, four distinct concepts have, at one time or another, been regarded as the prime aesthetic virture of arena staging. Most likely all arena theatres recognize and use some degree of all four. The remainder of this chapter will consider these notions that have come into fashion, will attempt to explain how they became accepted, and will point out the grounds on which each disappoints as a complete operating theory for arena staging.

1. The economic credential

The postwar readjustment period following World War II gave impetus to the sudden increase in arena staging in the United States. In the decade succeeding that war, almost like the notorious baby-boom, arena theatres doubled and redoubled in number. Prior to 1940 examples of theatre-in-the-round had been exotically rare and less than influential. Arch Lauterer suggests that the sudden surge in popularity was the result of something afloat in the feeling of the times which militated against an aging Broadway's decadent stranglehold on culture.[19] He surmised that after a war there ensues a period when people seem to dash for change, willy-nilly, with little forethought about the outcome.

One need not concur entirely with Mr. Lauterer to understand how, after a period of cataclysmic strife, an abundance of "angry" young folks eagerly parading "fresh" ideas for improving the future is apt to gather. A public voice, so long stilled, is bound at such times to seek vehicles of expression. Obviously, Broadway theatre, on sheer basic economics, alone could simply not absorb the influx of so many ambitious talents. It is almost embarrassingly simple to realize how conveniently the arena form might be tailored to permit entrepreneurs their entree. Here was a ready-made source of theatre whose economic feasibility allowed performing at the grass roots to seem an inviting enterprise. And since, to most, it was a relatively new and unknown form, it afforded an outlet for that adventurous pioneering spirit which promised a new order in the world. But to derogate the exuberant postwar "discovery" of arena theatre as an unworthy agent of random change, born of hapless economic expedience, appears to be an unwarranted indulgence in hasty cynicism. And time has not reflected kindly on Lauterer's views.

The leading champion of this early era was a true pioneer of professional arena theatre, Margo Jones. In the middle of her otherwise auspicious Broadway career, Miss Jones determined to establish her own resident, professional theatre in Dallas, Texas. In her famous book, *Theater-In-The-Round*, she declares unabashedly that had she been able to acquire appropriate space for a proscenium theatre, her world-renowned arena theatre would never have existed. The limitation of space and the pressure of economics coupled to convince her an arena theatre was her only recourse. There is no idealism here; the arena theatre was expedient. But in Margo Jones' "expedient" arena, the world was introduced to several important new plays by Tennes-

see Williams, William Inge, and Lawrence and Lee, which premiered
to rave critical notices in that lovely theatre.

Miss Jones' book begins with refreshing frankness; she notes
that the dream of theatre people in the 1950's was to establish a sort of
nation-wide theatre where all people could "find expression for their
art and craft as well as earn a livelihood."[20] Miss Jones' response to the
dream was based on simple economics: "The answer I have found in
Dallas, and which many theatre people are finding today lies in
theatre-in-the-round presentations."[21] The record, whether such facts
seem a cause for alarm or not, shows that the preponderance of arena
theatres in the 1940's and 1950's were born of this same "theatre-on-
the-cheap" motive. One must recall that, after all, in ancient tradition
theatres were improvised out of threshing floors by the Greeks, out of
open fields and wagons in the Middle Ages, out of innyards by the
Elizabethans, out of tennis courts by the French.... So why should the
arena movement be expected to fend off complaints about its humble
aspects?

Commercially, arena was favored for its novelty, at least for a
while. Television presently usurped that privilege. But at first
audiences were unaccustomed to seeing plays performed in their
midst, and the idea was marketable. Community groups, little theatres, schools and colleges no less than some professional companies
began to employ arena staging. One occasionally heard the rash
prediction that arena might eventually replace proscenium theatre
altogether. The music circus concept was born by St. John Terrell, in
Lambertville, New Jersey. It quickly rose in popularity throughout
the United States, and grew to a circuit of musical tent theatres from
coast to coast. Professional resident troupes also established houses
for dramatic theatre in adapted quarters, bringing live professional
seasons to New Orleans, Washington, D. C., Los Angeles, Houston,
Dallas, Chicago, Atlanta, Baltimore, Rochester, and many other
American cities. Accounting for the expansion of so much arena
activity can only be ascribed to its purported economic practicality.

The irony attendant to such an operating premise has already
been hinted at. A purely exploitative goal for arena is a pyrrhic
pursuit. One of its less apparent pitfalls turns out to have been that
true economy from arena theatre was actually a myth. While it is
correct that some costs of scenery can be avoided, costumes and other
items can no longer be acceptably faked and finally result in costs that
are much higher. However, the *most* deleterious effect of a threadbare
policy falls upon would-be, loyal, convinced patrons. Once the

novelty has worn off, there is little left to attract a public to a theatre whose outlook is to neglect artistic values. Audiences do not like to feel cheated. One could almost imagine hearing from members of arena audiences: "I miss the scenery and the mystery." It is wise not to ignore such comments. They may indicate that arena has failed to prove the vitality and importance of what replaces those elements; or, worse, they may mean that *nothing* has replaced them.

Economy will simply never suffice as an operating theory for production, neither in an arena nor anywhere else. And this is notwithstanding the professed ideals of Jerzy Grotowski's "Poor Theatre," which places great stress on high artistic achievement. Margo Jones, herself, seems cognizant of this very point when she states: "A new medium can be a challenge and a source of great theatrical excitement provided it is not cheapened to do the same old things in the same old ways."[22] Alas, her book fails to advise a better cause for people to employ arena theatre.

Often the dynamism and personal drive of people like Margo Jones have given sufficient impetus to sustain these theatres and allow them to thrive; and their endurance is more a testament to the personal driving force than to the arena form. Accounts of her Dallas theatre productions tend to verify that she insisted on top quality presentations.[23] Chances are that her talent and ability would have sustained her in any sort of theatre. If so, it is fair to conclude that economic expedience may serve to spread arena, but it fails miserably as a force to sustain it.

2. The intimacy combine

Having miscued with the principle of economy, arena practitioners hastened to come up with a better justification for their break with the traditional proscenium theatre. Arena quite eliminated the sort of scenic spectacle that had always entertained people so well. It pared most theatrical accounterments to the bone. What did it offer in their place?

Spectators in arena theatres almost universally agree that this method of production brings them closer to the action of the play, both in sheer physical proximity, then also psychologically. Arena artists jumped at this distinguished and apparent condition to reassert their artistic credentials. Their boast: The arena form returned the theatre to the people, by its new cognizance of audiences who were previously being treated like key-hole peepers as a result of the proscenium's fourth-wall convention. Arena provided a warm sense of intimacy, even camaraderie, between spectators and players.

Periodicals of the theatre were flooded with paeans to the theory of intimacy. One study surveying periodical literature notes seventeen articles appearing in United States journals alone, from 1947 to 1950, all touting the intimacy of arena theatre.[24] Brooks Atkinson, the distinguished *New York Times* theatre critic, was such an early partisan of arena theatre:

> Although most arena style theatres seem to derive
> from some practical, economic or housing problem, and
> are not intended as substitutes for the conventional stage,
> they have a positive virtue that cannot be duplicated. The
> audience has a complete sense of participation; it is drawn
> *intimately* into the spirit of the play and the acting.[25] [italics
> added]

His emphasis on the quality of intimacy later in the same article clearly illustrates how essential he felt it was to the character of arena performance. He asserted that arena theatres should necessarily be confined in size and capacity: "Too many people would destroy the intimacy and turn the arena style into an affectation."[26] Although Atkinson does not specifically define intimacy as the fundamental aesthetic characteristic of arena, as such, these statements leave little doubt as to the dominant influence he thought it had. Those whose shows Atkinson was reviewing very likely attributed similar importance to intimacy.

Indiscriminate enthusiasm for intimacy and acceptance of it as the keystone of arena practice, flourished for a time because no precise, unconditional definitions were demanded. Arena implied intimacy, to be sure; but did intimacy imply arena? The failure to formulate that question prevented people from realizing that, with intimacy, they had found nothing unique to arena theatre. Perhaps John Mason Brown came precipitously close to expressing that there was something more penetrating about arena than sheer intimacy when he wrote of a production at Margo Jones' theatre: "But the genuine and novel intimacy created by Miss Jones is not the result of the theatre's lack of size. It is the quite deliberate product of a seating-and-playing arrangement which alters—and alters utterly—the accepted relationship between spectators and actors."[27]

High overhead view, Model Portable Arena Theatre

Model Portable Arena Theatre: view from light battens.
Setting for "Chiaroscuro," by Louis Coppola

Exterior, Model, Portable Arena Theatre

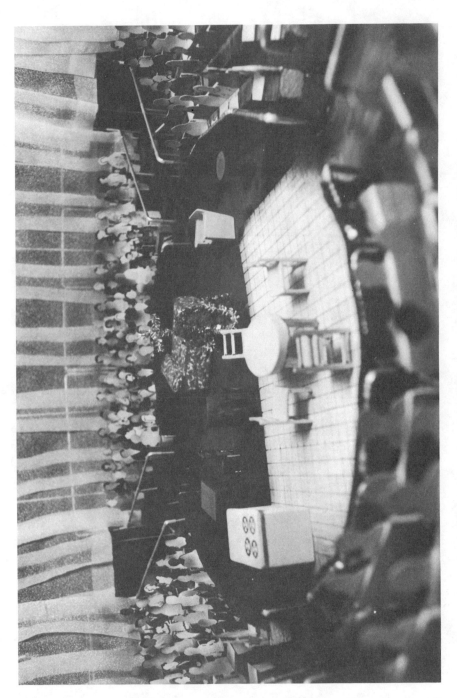

Audience view of stage and theatre, Model Portable Arena Theatre

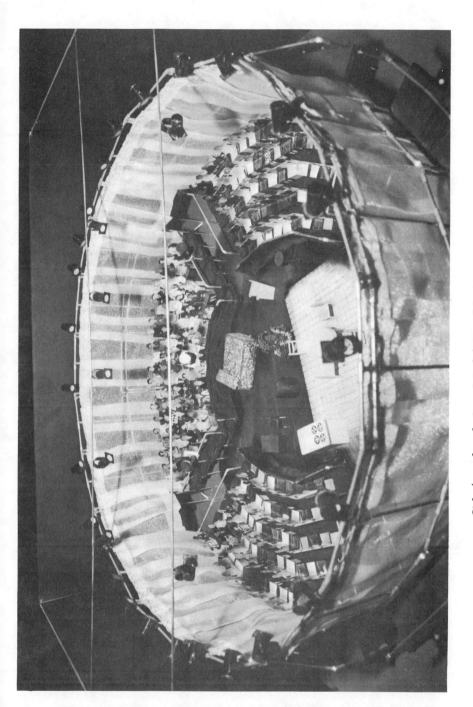

Side/overhead view, Model Portable Arena Theatre

As a basis on which to rationalize an operating theory, intimacy comes up short on two counts. First, arena is not the only form of intimate theatre. Many forms of theatre could claim similar power, and did. Proponents of flexible theatres were quick to point out that anything arena staging afforded in the way of intimacy could also be achieved from "less rigid theatre arrangements."[28] For all of that, even some of the old proscenium-style houses could boast a clear sense of intimacy. Second, too much intimacy might not be desirable. To tout intimacy as the arena's prime virtue is nearly to ignore the value of "psychical distance," a term made famous by the research of Edward Bullough.[29] Every arena theatre likely has at some time or other staged a production in which *distance* was momentarily lost, where audiences felt twinges of personal embarrassment during some particularly graphic love scenes, or perhaps violent audience reactions during scenes of strong emotional pitch. It is well to conclude then that intimacy is usually harder to avoid than to establish in a typical arena theatre, but it is not the basis of a special aesthetic principle on which such a theatre can uniquely operate.

3. The habit of representation

The third operational concept which controlled arena theatres was more nearly a *de facto policy* than a careful rational. Though the eagerness to feature intimacy was quietly shelved after it was apparent nothing unique was being offered, no new idea appeared as a ready substitute that could better account for arena practice. Most theatres pretty much continued to offer the same kinds of plays they were already dealing with. For the most part these were identical with what was being served out in the proscenium theatres of the day. Chiefly in the realistic mode, they were representational plays, that is, depicting supposedly real people in real circumstances. Where the box set on the proscenium stage had depicted a room with one wall removed, the arena merely asked audiences to imagine all four walls were removed. To assess the lists of productions which were offered from books like Margo Jones' *Theater-In-The-Round*, or Glenn Hughes' *The Penthouse Theater*, one would find representationalism (or plays so-described) predominant in those theatres through the early 1950's. The course of habit, rather than a rigorous doctrine, determined that arena theatres would operate as a representational medium, for it was unlikely that the bill of fare would differ much from the general average of plays done in New York or London, or in universities. It was the dominant mode of writers as well as theatres, at that time.

One scholarly study which admittedly spanned only a limited time-frame could be said to offer evidence of the prevailing policy. In *The Development of Arena Theatre in America as Reflected in Periodical Literature 1940-1950*, Martha Ann Koons states:

> By comparing the historic forms of staging with arena theater as defined, we see it is a new theater form. No other theater had an audience surrounding the acting area of a *representational, predominantly realistic* theater in which controlled lighting separates audience from actor.[30] [italics added]

Thirty years after that assessment, representational plays are still being staged in arena theatres, though few would care to argue that arena be limited to that mode of writing. The chief failing of such a policy is that it limits arena practice to a certain class of dramatic literature; whereas, experience demonstrates that other kinds of literature are just as viable for arena theatres.

A challenge to artists and students to shake off their lethargy was once again issued by theatre critic and historian, John Gassner. He reminded them: "It is very questionable that merely putting on a performance in the center of an auditorium is a 'style.' Stylization purely for reasons of expediency is not style; it fails to give specific character to a play."[31] Gassner's declaration obliges closer scrutiny. Just what sort of "style" was he hoping to see? In a personal response to the question, Mr. Gassner wrote me: "I must make it clear that I do not believe we must have *one* style, but we must have styles (in the choice of plays, and in the acting and staging of plays) *specially appropriate* to the special kind of arena theatre in use—if so-called arena-staging is to be more than a make-shift procedure."[32] The call to studious contemplation of arena theatre had finally been issued unequivocally. Now the challenge was truly made to arena's devotees to provide a serious rationale for their work.

4. The presentational response

Unlike the previous doctrines of artistic governance, a fourth theory about arena theatre took meticulous care to trace it as part of an historic sequence and to draw upon the precedence of earlier styles which would seem reasonably appropriate. From their scholarly research, some were impressed by the similarities they observed in the audience/actor relationship of integral arena theatre and those imputed to Greek theatres, Elizabethan "public" theatres, and even the stylized Chinese and Japanese theatres. All of these are regarded as "presentational" in character. Certainly one definition of presentation that goes along with the sense of offering a formal gift, particularly to the public, is the notion of aiming or directing an address by *facing* a particular direction. By contrast to representational theatre which tries to depict would-be persons or events as though they were really happening, this idea offers a performance which is unabashedly *in* and *of* the theatre, where there are actors, lights, and an audience. Presentationalism would not expect an audience to disbelieve (for the sake of fiction) it is attending the theatre; instead it would rejoice that it is present. Perhaps the epitome of modern presentationalism is to be found in Brecht's plays. Much of what passes in the name of presentationalism nowadays subscribes to the notion of trying to counter what its advocates claim is the "drugging" effect of illusion on audiences.

A doctoral dissertation by Joseph Golden marks the first real attempt in a full scholarly work to define the aesthetic character of the arena theatre. Reviewing the anti-realist doctrines from Appia to 1955, as well as comparing the modern arena theatre to the older theatrical forms previously mentioned, Golden believed an affinity exists between arena and those earlier concepts, which he regarded as predominantly theatricalist and presentational. From that he educed that modern arena should also be primarily a presentational medium. Fully cognizant that recent practice did not support his contention, it was still his considered opinion that realism was a mode unjustly imposed on arena theatre. Golden declares:

> We have observed the influence of this closeness and how it aids in creating an illusion of reality; extreme emphasis on acting that is natural, relaxed, yet concentrated; properties and settings that are correct, neat, and detailed. However, there are limitations both in theory and practice, limitations that affect acting, designing, lighting, and, of course, the viewing by the spectator.[33]

The fallacy in promulgating arena theatre as a presentational medium, however, is the same as regarding it as representational. Neither policy addresses what is unique about arena. Both conspire to promote a mode of dramaturgy. In doing so, they automatically limit the potential for arena to discover and foster other new modes. The theories are, then, self-serving. They do not afford a truly encompassing estimation of what is unique to arena theatre, which is, after all, what artists truly need to understand and deal with. Let there be representational drama, and let there be presentational drama; but where theatre-in-the-round employs them, let both benefit from being clothed with arena's own true aesthetic principles.

NOTES

I have chosen to cite Kenneth Macgowan's characterizations of the ideas of Adolph Appia, rather than going to the original sources. This was intentional, because Macgowan's interpretations were themselves catalysts that helped shape much of the emergent twentieth century arena theatre movement.

[1] Stephen Joseph, *Theater in the Round* (New York: Taplinger Publishing Company, 1967), p. 16.

[2] Suzanne K. Langer, *Feeling and Form* (New York: Charles Scribner's, 1953), p. 191.

[3] André Villiers, *Le Théâtre en Rond* (Paris: Librairie Théâtrale, 1958), p. 12.

[4] Arnold Haskell, *The Wonderful World of Dance* (Garden City, NY: Garden City Books, 1960), p. 14.

[5] Joseph, p. 17.

[6] Richard Southern, *The Medieval Theater in the Round* (New York: Theater Arts Books, 1975), p. 43.

[7] "A Sermon Against Miracle Plays," anon., *Dramatic Theory and Criticism* (New York: Holt, Rinehart and Winston, 1974), p. 112-17.

[8] Joseph, p. 26.

[9] Joseph, p. 28.

[10] Kenneth Macgowan and William Melnitz, *The Living Stage* (New York: Prentice Hall, 1955), p. 183-87.

[11] Oscar G. Brockett, *History of the Theatre* (Boston: Allyn and Bacon, Inc., 1960), p. 103.

[12] Macgowan and Melnitz, p. 435.

[13] Macgowan and Melnitz, p. 436.

[14] Edward Gordon Craig, *On the Art of the Theater* (New York: Theater Arts Books, 1960), p. 103.

[15] Brockett, p. 569.

[16] Arthur Hopkins, *Reference Point* (New York: Samuel French, 1948), p. 68-9.

[17] Charles Marowitz, *Stanislavski And The Method* (New York: Citadel Press, 1964), p. 155.

[18] See the following:

    [A] Henry Popkin, "The Drama Vs. the One-Ring Circus," Theater Arts, 35:39-42, February, 1951.

    [B] Arch Lauterer, "Speculations on the Value of Modern Theater Forms," NTC *Bulletin*, 11:11-18, December, 1949.

    [C] John Gassner, *The Theater In Our Times* (New York: Crown, 1954), p. 516-21.

    [D] Eric Bentley, *In Search Of Theater* (New York: Alfred A. Knopf, 1953), p. 382.

[19] Lauterer, "Speculations," p. 11, says: "The most distinctive changes in American Theater have followed each World War.... The failing in both periods of changes lies in the hasty use of borrowed ideas from European theater in a hurried effort to answer the need for more theaters."

[20] Margo Jones, *Theater-in-the-Round* (New York: Rinehart, 1951), p. 3.

[21] Jones, p. 5.

[22] Jones, p. 5. Also the following on page 12: "Much as I wanted to see theater flourishing across America, I want to state very firmly I believe bad theater is worse than no theater at all."

[23] John Rosenfield, "Dallas Theater '48," *Think*, April, 1948, p. 28-9.

[24] Martha Ann Koons, "The Development of Arena Theater in America As Reflected In Periodical Literature 1940-1950," (M.A. thesis, Pennsylvania State University, 1951), p. 72-127.

[25] Brooks Atkinson, "Arena Theater," *New York Times*, May 1, 1949, Sec. 2, p. 1.

[26] Atkinson, *ibid*.

[27] John Mason Brown, "In the Round," *Saturday Review of Literature*, 31:24-5, April 3, 1948.

[28] Kenneth Macgowan, "Theater in the Round," *New York Times*, March 21, 1948, Sec. 2, p. 1. Also see the following:

    [A] Walden Boyle, *Central and Flexible Staging* (Berkeley: University of California Press, 1956).

    [B] Ralph Freud, "Central Staging is Really Old Stuff," *Players Magazine*, December, 1948, p. 52-3.

[29] Edward Bullough, "Psychical Distance as a Factor in Art and an Aesthetic Principle," *British Journal of Psychology*, June, 1912.

[30] Koons, p. 155.

[31] Gassner, *In Our Times*, p. 518.

[32] Based on personal correspondence between Dr. John Gassner, Stirling Professor of Playwriting at Yale University, and the writer, November, 1956.

[33] Joseph Golden, "The Position and Character of Theater in the Round in the United States," (Ph.D. dissertation, University of Illinois, 1956).

THE CRITICAL REEXAMINATION

A flaw found in common among theories developed to guide the practice and understanding of arena theatre has been their failure to equip arena with a conspicuously "unique" style, that is, to afford arena production some faculty which is unattainable in any other medium. Plays are staged in the round not so much because doing so is crucial to accomplish the particular work, but rather for various less-than-artistic reasons. No plays are written which rely on a theatre's roundness to articulate their cogence. None of the theories, to date, has been fertile enough to disclose arena's essence. When past attempts were made to come to serious grips with arena theatre, each began by inquiring: What is known about such staging? Hence, they strained to educe an operational theory from an historical perspective. That approach inevitably informed us how arena could be likened to other more familiar models of theatre; so it tends to disguise, rather than clarify, vital philosophic distinctions which cause arena to be a unique medium. Writings about arena have all too frequently made apologies for such differences. What is wanted is a passionate espousal of just those differences because they do something altogether unique, altering the very essence of theatre. As things stand, probably few artists, given free choice, would deliberately select pure arena theatre to create their work. Indeed, not many artists realize even what it is that is "created" in arena theatre. Current preference tends to lean toward more traditional forms, which may be better understood and so more thoroughly exploited, because artists find them safer, and feel more secure in familiar forms.

Numerous creative matters underpin the making of art works for the arena theatre. By examining them it is possible to address the issues of the creative artist, rather than to focus on the typical historian's concerns, to the end that the unique features, problems, and inherent opportunities to be found in arena theatre can be observed as well. Such an approach additionally provides an insight into the historical and philosophical significance of the arena medium as it relates to a modern age.

One of the foremost theorists on aesthetics and philosophy of the arts has been Susanne K. Langer. Her work provides a useful comprehensive artistic and aesthetic guideline and must form the basis of any discussion.*

SECTION ONE: Setting the Aesthetic Ground Rules

In the examination of arena theatre, certain basic concepts regarding all art must be introduced for the convenience of common terminology if for no other reason. Two concepts, in particular, are vital and may be phrased as questions: What does art create? How does such a creative process differ from other activities? Ultimately, the creation of unique works of art in arena theatres is the prize we seek; Langer launches that quest by specifying what is created in art, itself: "Art is the creation of forms symbolic of human feelings."[1] In that short dictum, Langer encompasses her philosophy of what art means, and upon that statement, a useful theory of arena theatre may be constructed.

The "art symbol"

Artistic significance, which is to say, the "import" of art, is an issue of tangible concern for anyone who hopes to succeed in recognizing *how* and *when* significant expression can occur, especially within arena theatres. Fortunately, such significance becomes uniquely discernible when one understands Langer's simple, though profound, concept of the "art symbol." She divulges a key to this insight through drawing a crucial distinction in art between "signs" or "signals" on the one hand, versus "symbols" on the other: "A signal is comprehended if it serves to make us notice the object or situation it bespeaks. A symbol is understood when we conceive the idea it presents."[2] Simplistically stated, her point might be glimpsed by recognizing that, for instance, a traffic light obviously serves as a *signal* to stop or go, yet simultaneously functions at a deeper level of awareness as a *symbol* of the idea or concept of safety.

---

* Because Langer's ideas are clearly and succinctly stated, it is often necessary to cite her completely. Any paraphrase or attempt to fragment her words is inadequate to sustain her valuable contributions to theatre theory.

Distinctions between "signals" and "symbols" become increasingly more cogent when how they apply to art works is ascertained. Any work of art, unquestionably, may express its author's mere state of mind at the moment of its creation, or might illustrate some of his beliefs—political, scientific, or whatever. Moreover, such a work could perhaps show the social or cultural milieu of his epoch. Even the author's dreams or nightmares may find expression in the work. However, each of these things might be detected equally well in every sort of drawing, utterance, gesture, or personal record of any kind whatsoever. As ingredients, they will never constitute the *essence* of artistic expression. Each is merely a "signal" or symptom of some actual fact or object. To create works of art, whether in arena theatres or elsewhere, artists must evoke some awareness deeper than mere "signals" or symptoms of actuality.

Langer vigorously exhorts us to realize that "the function of art, like that of science, is to acquaint the beholder with something he has not known before... the artistic symbol, *qua* artistic, negotiates insight, not reference; it does not rest upon conventions, but motivates and dictates conventions."[3]   Next Langer espouses her view that the significance of art arises out of its *expression of an idea*. Insofar as this may be similar to discourse (it is *not* altogether similar, she explains) the function of such expression is *symbolic*, i.e., the "articulation and presentation of concepts."[4] Therefore, when Langer declares that art creates forms symbolic of human feelings, her literal meaning is that art creates forms which "articulate" and "present" concepts of human feelings. Art never merely *signals* (refers to) human feelings. A work of art presents feeling (in the broad sense—everything that can be felt) for our contemplation, making it visible or audible in some way perceivable through a symbol, not inferable from a symptom.   A "symbol" is any device whereby an abstraction can be made.

Parsing her rather cerebral, didactic response to those several initial questions, profound implications may be drawn here for arena theatre: Primarily, one should deduce this axiom: AN ARENA PLAY'S "FORM" MUST SYMBOLIZE ("articulate and present a concept of") HUMAN FEELINGS. Indeed, to become art works whatsoever, arena plays must not function simply as referents (signals) to human feelings.   That is a key precept.   There is also a corollary: Whatever symbolic form our play may take, it cannot "rest on borrowed conventions, but will" (being a symbolic structure) "dictate its own."

Artistic creation

Langer's observation that artistic expression has this uniquely symbolic motive, reasserts for art its claim to "creativity." Her aesthetics propound that something is decidedly "created" in art; this rebuts all those who maintain that art is merely a sort of *re-creation*. Frequently theatre people, faced with doing plays on an arena stage, are culpable of approaching their task as though the job implied "re-creating" a work originally devised for some other sort of theatre. In response to this, Langer cautions:

> The word "creation" is introduced here with full awareness of its problematical character. There is a definite reason to say a craftsman *produces* goods, but *creates* a thing of beauty; a builder *erects* a house, but *creates* an edifice if the house is a real work of architecture, however modest. An artifact as such is merely a combination of natural parts, or a modification of natural objects to suit human purposes. It is not a creation but an arrangement of given factors. A work of art, on the other hand, is more than an arrangement of given things, even qualitative things. Something emerges from that arrangement of tones and colors, which was not there before, and this, rather than the arranged material is the symbol of sentience.[5]

Her argument clearly sheds new light on one prickly critique concerning arena staging by the late John Gassner. He once warned arena practitioners: "Merely ordering the actors to enable every spectator to see them from time to time cannot assure expressiveness in a production. . . . Nothing can do more harm to the art of staging plays than to turn the stage director into a new kind of traffic-cop."[6] Gassner's barb, which is probably a more-valid indictment of practices today than it even was almost thirty years ago, can also be understood when stated in Langer's vocabulary as "a mere arrangement of given factors." Plainly, productions which endure such "traffic-copping" are doomed to be mere *artifacts*. The arrangement of actors for the purpose of being seen by various flanks of audience is nothing if not an arrangement "to suit human purposes" and implies an old proscenium theatre premise—that each spectator shall see the same thing, and at the same time—an ideal eventually achieved only cinematically, and at most only approximated by proscenium theatres.

Transcending such mediocrities, however, is the way by which arena plays *do* become artistic creations, and through a recognition of the art symbol lies the touchstone. A work enters the realm of creativity and becomes a work of art through "symbolic" constructs; these may, but need not necessarily, be managed with a skillful degree of craft.

The image as symbol

That "something" which *emerges* from the arrangement of the raw materials, (Langer earlier referred to it as the "symbol of sentience,") is the *salient ingredient* that is vital to any new examination of arena theatre. The process which transforms raw materials into the realm of art is something common to all the arts, after all, the creative process. Langer evokes a discussion of it like this: "What is created in a work of art? More than people usually realize. . . . It is an image, created for the first time out of things that are not imaginal, but quite realistic—canvas or paper, and paint, or carbon, or ink."[7] Or the thousand and one elements artists employ in creating art works in genres different from the graphic arts , primarily three: *space, spoken language, and the human form.* The creative process through which the *images* of incipient arena artists can emerge out of these several raw materials is of particular importance.

As long as there has been theatre, people have striven to create images. However, it was Langer who convincingly detailed the symbolic—in contrast to the mere signaling—nature of such images. And in doing so, she has advanced a clearer understanding of the inner workings of the arts. Langer's innovative elucidation of the art symbol clearly untangles one debilitating paradox that for years beclouded the efforts of arena partisans to rationally describe the intrinsic nature of the arena medium.

The Paradox and its resolution

Ever since Aristotle first attributed the concept of "imitation" to the dramatic artist, a debate has raged: Theatre-people, as well as various western philosophers, have grappled around, trying to figure out what constitutes the proper admixture of *real* factors (e.g., the players, the stage, the spectacle, the poem, the audience, etc.) to communicate vital dramatic images. Theatre history has become a virtual testament to the age-old conflict over what should be the correct relationship between an image and its *real* model. Arena theatre found itself ensnared on the horns of this debate when previous theories meant to explain arena's nature (i.e., the rival doctrines of representationalism vs. presentationalism) got bogged down over barren, diversionary claims for realism, or its alter ego, theatricalism.

Echoes of Naturalism

Prominent among the historical epochs that hotly pursued a flawed ideal was the era of Naturalism. The school of Naturalism is often epitomized by the writings of André Antoine or the stage productions of David Belasco. The work of such men gave impetus to the concept: the "imitation of reality," sometimes also coined as "the slice of life." Throughout theatre history, early as well as late, the sort of approach evinced by the naturalists could also be noted in others. For instance, the powerful sway of copying the real is surely responsible for notorious distortions with so-called "Method" acting. Naturalism, seen in one of its derivative modes as representationalism, bore heavily upon the early theoretics and practice among arena theatres.

Few people today fail to appreciate that Naturalism became obsessed with the "real." From hindsight we find it almost ludicrous that Naturalists wished to exactly replicate objects of their intended imagery. People cite one Belasco work so often that it has become a cliché. His brick by brick reconstruction of a Schrafft's Restaurant for a stage set is perhaps *the* best known example of such a naturalistic impulse run amok. The pitfall to such fastidious absorption with the real and actual was that spectators eventually became so engrossed with these actual elements they lost regard for the values of what was being expressed. The art "symbol" was forsaken for a mere "signal."

Fall-out of Anti-illusion

No less confused, although in today's climate of theatre more recalcitrant, are the "anti-illusionists" who are still confounded over the proper relationship between image and model. These are "revanchists" against the school of Naturalism. While in their counteractivity this group ridiculed the bogey "imitation of reality," in effect they merely replaced it with another substitute set of realities. Whereas they virulently rejected dramaturgy that professed to copy nature, they are themselves as inept as the Naturalists at dealing with the

symbolic function of art. They, too, are preoccupied with signals
(symptoms). They insist that actors are, frankly, actors, the stage is
indisputably a stage, and the audience is unequivocally an audience;
they require us all to remain incessantly aware of *these* mundane
actualities. Brechtian techniques of alienation, purporting to dispel
illusionism, for a time became all the modern rage; nowadays theatre-
people appreciate that such alienations were not effected quite as
Brecht literally described. Rather we now concede that Brecht actually
created secondary illusions,[8] and, in effect, gave a new twist to an
ancient contrivance—a play within a play. Meanwhile, this cult of
anti-illusionists entrapped themselves with rubrics as ill-conceived as
the Naturalists'. And unfortunately, anti-illusion theoretics pressed a
self-proclaimed right to subjugate arena practice entirely, insisting
this was its native habitat.

Joseph Golden's treatise advocating anti-illusionism for arena
theatres should be recalled. In approaching the topic of frequently-
touted intimacy in arena theatres, Golden began his objections, "We
have observed this closeness and how it aids in creating an illusion of
reality...."[9] Those strange words, "*illusion* of reality," appear to have
become the *bête noire* in his thesis. He was disenchanted by such
"illusions of reality" (whatever that means) seen ubiquitously in
representationalistic arena productions.

This curious phrase recurs throughout his book. He complains
of the arena stage designer, "He may achieve some illusion of reality,
but the illusion is only partial."[10] He further alleges, "Actors in realistic
plays are frankly imitators of 'real' people...."[11] Such generalizing
scarcely conceals a strain of bias. To consummate his rationalization
that arena is inherently anti-illusionistic, Golden pronounces, "By
making audiences more conscious of themselves and the techniques
of realistic production, complete illusion on the arena is almost impossible."[12]

Misguided inferences about arena are inevitable, of course, if
one postulates that "*imitation* of reality" and "*illusion* of reality" are
somehow the same concept—that they both mean "copying," or
"replicating" actuality. Golden plainly misconstrues the fallacy in
naturalism, or its realistic heirs. Naturalism does not attempt to create
"*illusions* of reality," as his unfortunate diction might suggest; rather,
it tries to express reality with *reality*,"—a mere signal, a "*delusion*."
Ironically, anti-illusionism goes afoul over exactly the same error.
Langer has also addressed this issue with care and precision, and
ultimately differentiates that *illusion* and *reality* must never be linked

as one concept, since their functions remain essentially quite contrary:

> The philosophical issue that is usually conceived in
> terms of image and object is really concerned with the
> nature of images as such and their essential differences
> from actualities. The difference is functional; consequently
> real objects, functioning in a way that is normal for images,
> may assume a purely imaginal status. That is why the
> character of an *illusion* may cling to works of art that do not
> represent anything. Imitation of other things is not the
> power of images, though it is a very important one by
> which the whole problem of fact and fiction originally
> came into the compass of our philosophical thought. But
> the true power of an image lies in the fact that it is an
> abstraction, a symbol, the bearer of an idea.[13] [italics
> added]

To reconcile with this point, one must understand that illusions
are simply images. By basic inference, therefore, one may conclude
there is nothing necessarily inimical in any artistic sense about an
arena theatre which is either realistic or theatricalistic, provided, of
course, that either accomplishes its greater aim: namely, to convey an
abstraction, a symbol.

This resolves a quarrelous paradox because all partisan ideolo-
gies about whether arena should be regarded as intrinsically more
realistic or more theatrical are simply moot. The artist's crucial
concern is that arena should not merely draw its spectators' attention,
or refer them, to its *materials*. Rather, it must convey to them a *symbolic
idea*. These materials of arena theatre, whether one is alluding to actual
bricks or actual actors, must successfully take on an imaginal status,
and articulate a concept of human feeling. Abstracted out of the
context of the real world, as *illusions*, these materials bear a new idea.
Langer states, "An image in this sense, something that exists only for
perception, abstracted from the physical, causal order, is the artist's
creation."[14]

Illusion is the catalyst

What is paramount for arena artists is to establish that "illusion"
is what constitutes all art. Instead of confusing that term with
replication, or all those pejorative connotations of fraudulence which
have somehow attached to it, one should appreciate the valid role of

illusion in art. Illusion is not about something actual; instead, it is virtual. While the character of an illusion may in some cases, though not always, be imitative, its function is to dissociate for the beholder the virtual image created in a work of art from its actual, mundane environment; not to absorb him into that actual environment. Langer reminds us, "Even when the element of representation is absent, when nothing is imitated or feigned—in a lovely textile, a pot, a building, a sonata—the air of illusion, of being a sheer image, exists as forceably as in the most deceptive picture or the most plausible narrative."[15]

It is precisely at the point when the spectator is least caught up in the physical factors in a work of art that he fixes his thoughts neither upon the paint nor the canvas; that is, when his attention singles out neither the people acting, nor the bricks, nor the stage, nor the technical apparatuses of the theatre, that he is best able to observe the work's sheer appearance as such, that is, its semblance, its illusion. This is not a game of "make believe" but rather Coleridge's familiar concept of the "willing suspension of disbelief."

Arena artists must go about finding ways to develop "illusions" using the materials which arena affords them. Among the attitudes which often constrict imaginations, and conspire against artists contemplating to work with arenas is the tendency to consider images as only *visual* things. Langer deplores such lack of comprehension, cautioning, "Many people . . . regard an image or illusion as something necessarily visual."[16] Yet dramatic arts can command a panoply of images—poetic, kinesthetic, musical, or many more; each of these can communicate its own semblance of life. Each has its special way of symbolizing *living form*. Once artists grasp the quintessential nature of the materials arena can provide and recognize the profound import which can be wrought by such imaginative manipulation, arena should be ripe to experience a vigorous resurgence. Arena has its special way to symbolize *living human form*. Langer exhorts: "To produce and sustain the essential illusion, set it off from the surrounding world of actuality, and articulate its form to the point where it coincides unmistakably with forms of feeling and living, is the artist's task."[17]

SECTION TWO: The Reexamination

With Langer's blueprint examination of the aesthetic aim of all the arts thus established, it is possible to proceed to an analysis of the empirical phenomenon of arena theatre by inquiring what it alone creates. Differences and similarities between the "real factors," the raw materials, as it were, employed by both arena and other staging methods must be considered as well. Theodore Shank advises: "A work of art is an illusion which its materials and techniques have created; it is not the sum of the commonplace materials which have gone into its making."[18] A most important part of the examination involves the malleability of space in arena staging, the manner in which it is used, and the way in which it is formed; yet the task of "creating illusions of living form" remains to be carried out by working arena artists. Shank cautions: "The arts should not be defined by the materials and techniques they use, but by what these are used to create."[19]

Raw materials are defined by Theodore M. Greene as "Whatever might be of use to the artist for ultimate manipulation and interpretation, considered prior to all preliminary selection and organization."[20]

Without exception, the raw materials of arena theatre coincide with those of all the dramatic arts. A play in arena requires actors to play the roles, a script or some subject matter to be performed, illumination, artificial or natural, that is sufficient for the spectators to perceive the action, and space to contain the action. Also the ornaments of spectacle could be included: costumes, fabrics, props, furnishing, settings, sound effects. Although these are in no way strictly essential, in the overall sense of theatre these could still be considered as raw materials.

What distinguishes arena from other types of theatre, then, is not its general materials, but one specific type of material: its medium. Greene offers this definition of a medium: "The artistic medium is the same material (as the raw material) *after* it has been selected and organized in such a way as to be immediately available for artistic use."[21] The *space* of arena theatres is a unique medium in exactly the sense that watercolors or acrylic paints are each media of the graphic arts. Anyone hoping to employ arena felicitously ought to appreciate the nature of arena's spatial characteristics for imaginative manipulation.

Putting a play into the arena medium literally means putting it into an "especially selected and organized kind of space." Such spaces as this "alter utterly—the accepted relationship between spectators and actors,"[22] as John Mason Brown once perceptively discerned. It is the *unique* feature which differentiates arena from all other theatre media.

Let us now examine this difference in detail by using diagrams to illustrate ground-plans for various kinds of stages.

A. The proscenium-arch theatre

In Figure 2, notice that an actor is placed in approximately the center stage position, simply as a point of reference. From such a reference location the actor may move about in his surrounding space.

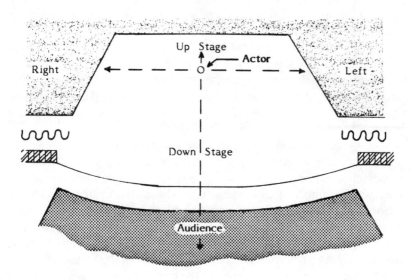

Figure 2
The Audience/Actor Relationship in Proscenium Theatre.

The first possibility of movement is on a horizontal axial plane, which is to say he may move left or right. Essentially such left/right movements will not alter perceptibly the focal relationship between his role and the audience. The "meaning" of his horizontal moves for the audience are tied exclusively to points in the fiction, the play. A move in a right or left direction is determined solely by what the fiction constructs as the *meaning* of stepping out in that direction: perhaps he is going toward the city or toward the next room.

The other basic axis of movement, upstage/downstage, becomes quite a different matter, however. Movements by the actor along the upstage/downstage axis assume a supervening "meaning" which is *not* constructed through the fiction. By coming downstage the actor changes his focal plane and draws decidedly more attention to himself; when he retreats upstage, this attention diminishes. This extraneous claim upon the upstage/downstage axis imposes artificial restraints upon such movements. Even when stepping toward an upstage door might "mean" going toward another room—a construct of the fiction—it is likewise a hostage to the non-fictionally imposed, hence artificial, condition which all such movement carries, namely, a diminished focal attention.

To be sure, there are compositional tricks which can offset these conditions, but this is not the point. The fact remains that such fundamentally arbitrary conditions impose upon any movement the actor attempts to make on the proscenium stage. Rules, not constructed out of the psychological action of the play, but out of the artificial requisites of picturization which this sort of stage imposes, take governance upon the expression of the subject.

For certain types of plays such artificial up- and downstage movements can be ideal; for example, when it is necessary that actors dominate or step out of a scene to address the audience. This is undoubtedly the reason why lecture platforms are nearly always situated so that the speaker may keep his back toward one wall and face his audience, which is more or less opposite him. Paradoxically, this underlying principle runs counter to many of the historic notions about proscenium-arch theatre. In the era usually thought to be the highest refinement of the proscenium-arch theatre—that of the box-setting—the use of its up/downstage axis was thwarted, subject to the rigors of the fourth-wall convention. Yet whether the realists obstructed all movement at the curtain line or not, the indelible fact persists: proscenium theatre operates under innate laws of an artificial determinant, the up/downstage axis. Contrary to the ideas of nineteenth century inventors of box-settings, and reason for twentieth century disciples of the tradition to take pause, is this evidence that proscenium theatre by the nature of its artificial rules superimposes artifice upon realism. The fourth-wall convention was a clear and drastic compromise with intrinsic aesthetic characteristics of the proscenium-arch theatre.

B. The open stage

Figure 3 is a diagram of a typical open stage. It is similar to the Elizabethan stage, and is sometimes questionably referred to as a three-quarter or thrust arena. The actor may now move in the space of this stage in different ways. The left/right axis remains with its "fictional" basis intact. Left may still "mean" going toward the city, and

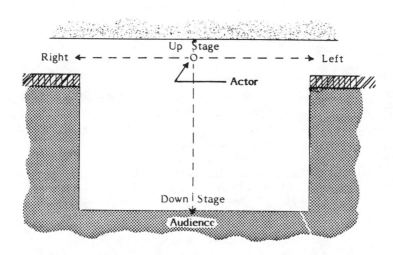

Figure 3
An Open Stage

the right to Capulet's home. Also the same features of the up/
downstage apply. Some believe these features are even more powerful on the open stage where the physical impedimenta of set flats and
grand-drape curtains are taken away. Richard Southern, in his book,
Open Stage, describes in vivid passages the actor making a direct
address to the audience:

> He advances downstage and he begins to speak as he
> moves. But he advances all the time. He walks past the
> place where, in a picture-frame theater, the footlights
> would be. And he continues. He walks over the position
> of the orchestra, and over the front row of stalls and over
> the second. Still he advances, coming right out into the
> theater, over the third row, and the fourth and the fifth.
> Now he is half way out to us, still speaking, and our eyes
> are on him. He holds us to the complete exclusion of the
> group behind, which can distract in no sense; it is in
> another focus. And then he stands, but his speech goes on,
> coming to us from the center of our world, addressed to all
> around him—a peak moment of the banquet scene, not a
> hold up in it. And he speaks as he would wish to—out and
> away from the world of gossip which he scorns, and enjoy-
> ing his secession, gives us his comments on all cocktail
> parties and at last walks away, half-smiling at them, upon
> his own devices; and a new dimension of theater has been
> achieved.[23]

Since preponderant evidence indicates that Elizabethans staged
many of their plays using this very arrangement, it seems prudent to
suggest that the new dimension Southern acclaims here is more precisely just an old dimension restored. There is a telling remark in this
regard at the outset of Southern's book:

> The key to these four papers is the wish to see the
> urgent figures of modern drama served by an adequate
> acting-place. The figures, for instance, in the plays of Eliot,
> Anouilh, Cocteau, Fry . . . figures and plays of modern
> drama also have a strange urgency which at present is
> irresolutely unreconciled to the conditions and limitations
> of our contemporary stage. They won't fit. They struggle
> out of it; they are too exuberant or too portentous for it.[24]

The formal parallels between Elizabethan plays and those by
the men Southern has mentioned here are obvious. Each of these
playwrights has a strong predilection for either soliloquy or verse;
both devices normally warrant presentational delivery (direct ad-

dress to the audience). Even if there are countless ways to suppress or circumvent this fundamental characteristic, eventually one must reconcile with the urgent sense that the open stage is ideally suited to presentational theatre.

C. The nearly-encircled stage

Certain intermediate configurations exist in theatre architecture which provide variations on all designs. Some arrangements might place an audience on two sides of the stage, either adjacently or at opposite ends. Others might place a rectangular staging area between two audience areas, or the stage might be in a corner with the audience surrounding it in a triangular fashion. Figure 4, for example, presents a hypothetical arrangement which is somewhat more radical than the traditional thrust stage where the audience is seated on three sides of a rectangular or square stage. This illustration presents a stage

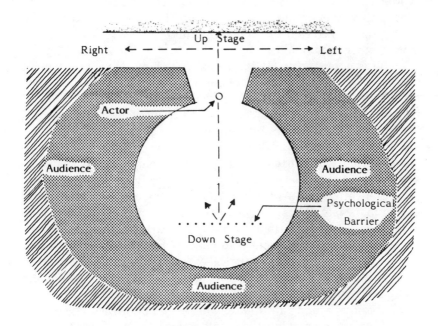

Figure 4
Actor nearly encircled by Audience

that is nearly completely encircled by the audience with only a small portion of the audience ring left open for scenic pieces, entrances, and exits.

Radical and hypothetical as this illustration might be, however, it is no less improbable a theatrical design than the Ruth Taylor Theatre at Trinity University in San Antonio, Texas, wherein the director, Paul Baker, called in the late seventies for a three-stage design that almost completely encircled the audience and allowed for continuous and simultaneous action to take place on all stages while the audience was seated in swivel chairs that allowed them to turn first one way and then another in order to follow the course of the productions from stage to stage. Such a design as Baker's worked well (it was first constructed at Baylor University in Waco, but that was a modified proscenium theatre; whereas, the Ruth Taylor was specifically designed to meet Baker's special criteria) for such productions as his award-winning *Hamlet* which used three actors playing the title role at the same time in order to illustrate the ambivalent nature of the Prince's character and questionable madness.

Subsequent experiments involving *Macbeth* and Thornton Wilder's *The Skin of Our Teeth* were not as well received by the constantly swiveling and turning audiences; however, the experimental staging worked well for *Twelfth Night* and *The Caucasian Chalk Circle* among other productions.

It is noteworthy, however, that following Baker's retirement from Trinity University, subsequent directors have not utilized the three-stage, audience encircled concept to any degree whatever, and the prototype of the design at Baylor University has been reconverted to a standard proscenium auditorium. Margo Jones, a former student and later associate of Paul Baker's, also worked on Baker's three-stage concept when directing at Baylor and occasionally at Trinity University in San Antonio. Her theatrical philosophy, expressed largely through her instruction of classes at Trinity and at the Dallas Theatre Center in the late sixties and early seventies, suggested that the value of theatrical staging lay in innovation and experimentation. In this, she was clearly in agreement with Baker, who served as mentor and teacher for any number of theatrical artists for over two decades.

Returning to the example in Figure 4, while considerably less attention is drawn to it than in the previous diagrams, the last vestiges of a horizontal action path still remain. Even now an actor could exit out to the right or left. Only the events assigned in the fiction offer any particular significance to either direction. But has the upstage/

downstage axis changed? Is it still possible for an actor to take a commanding view of his entire audience and deliver a speech to all simultaneously?

Although it may be slightly more uncomfortable than before, it can still be done. If the actor were to situate himself midway between the banks of audience on either side of the open end, he *may* address all around him in a single sweeping glance, without turning his back to anyone. The curious factor, however, is what happens when the actor advances in a downstage direction, still trying to deliver the same speech. After passing the half-way point and coming on down about three-quarters of the distance, he begins to sense automatically an intensifying impulse to turn on his heels and speak to those behind. Richard Southern described this very impulse in operation on a stage rather less radically enclosed, even, than the one in Figure 4:

> One word should be said about John English's so-called Arena Theater. It possesses what I might call a square stage with a semi-circle added to the front of it. This is all only a few inches high and the audience sits in one unbroken amphitheater around front and sides. The curious experience is that as one advances slowly down stage from back to front one feels all the normal impressions of advancing on an open stage—but only to a certain point on the floor. That point is where the center of the circle upon which the auditorium is struck occurs, and it is roughly at a place where what I have called the square area of the stage abuts the fronting semi-circular area. Beyond this point one advances only to find a quite strong inclination to revolve on one's axis and play with one's back to the audience.[25]

Whereas this theatre in Birmingham, England, which Southern has described here is by no means an integral arena theatre, in any purist's definition, one can begin to discern from its example the implications that begin to dawn as the ever-greater enclosure of the stage by audience begins to take place. We now stand at the threshold of realizing the specific, intrinsic arena impulse.

D. Integral arena theatre

Figure 5 shows a diagram of a typical arena theatre floor plan. While there are a number of shapes to arena stages other than the

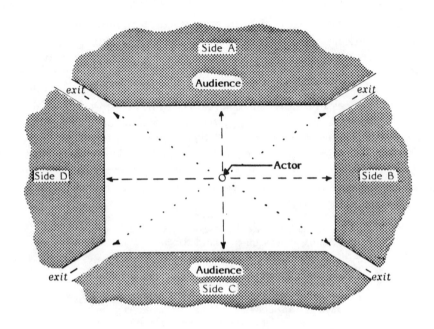

Figure 5
An Integral Arena Theatre

rectangle depicted here, integral arena stages are always completely ringed in or encapsulated by the percipients, except for entrance aisles. No single geometric form seems to have gained universal approval for arena stages, though the majority are rectangular. This may have evolved as much from architectural exigency as from any deliberate selection by those alleging a superior aesthetic quality to the rectangular form. However, among arena theatres featuring something other than rectangular stages, a safe assumption is that the alternative *was* selected as a result of conscious preference. For instance, at the Tufts Arena Theater in Boston, Massachusetts, an elliptical-shaped stage was built to the particular specifications of its founders. *Le Théâtre en Rond* in Paris, has a circular stagespace. Its artistic director, André Villiers, has written a meticulous rationale supporting his adherence to the "perfect circle." *Teatro Sant' Erasmo* in Milan, Italy had a nearly octagonal playing space. Margo Jones' Theater-in-the-Round in Dallas used a stage which was very nearly a regular trapezoid.

Since all these shapes seem to work suitably, whichever geometric pattern is selected apparently amounts to an expressive nuance of greater concern to individual arena producers, than to the viability of the medium over-all. The one non-optional characteristic that remains crucial, however, is having a stage fully surrounded by the audience.

What is the relationship of actor to audience once they surround him from all sides? How can our actor now possibly deliver a speech frontally to all audience members simultaneously? Unless he were to join the ranks of the whirling dervishes, his only possible station is to go into an entrance aisle; nowhere else would he be able to encompass them all at a glance. The "fact" of this irrevocable situation, which proves a dismaying absence of imperious stage loci, can be witnessed any time a master of ceremonies strides out onto an arena stage. One could scarcely find any more ill-serving platform from which to deliver a direct speech or presentation. Moreover, the positions at the head of entrance aisles are almost equally as unsuitable. Most such aisles are rather narrow, by definition, so the speaker seems to blend right in with the surrounding audience. This is surely an unfavorable place for one to try to draw and command concerted attention to oneself. Hence arena theatre beggars material whose expression is contingent upon *artificial* (attention-assuming) axes.

Some artists grumble that this distinguishing feature becomes a limitation, since they persistently think of theatre as being action in composed pictures, albeit pictures in motion. Conversely, however, arena might just liberate the artist from the phoney rigors of composed perspective which have confined him for too many centuries to presenting a contrived and artificial semblance of life.

It is of no small importance to recognize what this means—that arena space HAS NO PRESENTATIONAL AXIS; all other sorts of theatre, including amphitheatres, motion pictures, television, or what you will, obviously have a presentational axis. This is why such pains have been exercised to literally observe the distinctions.[26] Southern cautions open stage proponents to heed the differences:

> We have however to distinguish between pure arena work and open-stage presentation. The lack of background of any sort in arena makes it a special theater problem . . .[27]

Once every trace of a perspective-oriented up/downstage axis has dissolved and is supplanted by the three-dimensional medium of arena and the actor has been freed from a contrived, focally warped set of rules dictated by pictorial composition, then the ring of a critically-examining audience can fully encircle the dramatic event, effectively blocking the actor's retreat into the old order. A new and radical complexion emerges to alter the conception of theatre itself. Whereas, former perceptions were limited only to pictographic and visual images which encumbered concepts of human feeling and even an understanding of life with all the clutter of convention requisite to pictorial perspective, now arena theatre can challenge and demand a reorientation of the notion of how artistically to express and understand the human dilemma.

Implications from the graphic arts

To avoid artistic chaos which might arise form this disconcerting new freedom, it is urgent to contemplate the differences between pictorial space and round space. Langer remarks:

> The illusion created in pictorial art is a *virtual scene*. I do not mean a "scene" in the special sense of "scenery"—the picture may represent only one object or even consist of pure decorative forms without any representational value—but it always creates a space opposite the eye and related directly and essentially to the eye. That is what I call "scene."[28]

Any stage or other medium which intrinsically features a presentational axis creates by definition the illusion of a *virtual scene*. Any such medium places the actor *philosophically* in a space opposite the eye and related directly and essentially to the eye. The audience witnesses the action in terms of *scene*, and even when the actor comes forward out of the scene to speak directly to the audience, he is nonetheless related visually to it. From the first, the ruling conception of the piece has been in terms of composed visual images. Theatre people have been ingrained in the tradition of imagining drama as an enactment in a *virtual scene*. This concept has become fixated for them, almost to the point of atrophying their powers of discernment, through the ubiquitous mechanical media—film and television. Could anything prove more self-contradictory or incongruous, for example, than attempting to render arena performances on film or television? Yet more and more, just such self-negating aberrations show up, particularly on television.

Dramatic artists are not the only ones who have been baffled by ways to achieve expression in a third dimension, although they have been painfully slow about trying for clear answers. Langer mentions a sculptor and theorist named Hildebrand who once tried to explain his medium in essentially pictorial terms when he wrote *The Problem of Form in Painting and Sculpture*.[29] She notes that he apparently "carried over the concept of pictorial space, lock, stock and barrel..."[30] and was caught up in the same sort of miscalculations which commonly confound theatre artists. Langer cautions:

> This is far too simple a way to pass from a special theory of pictorial space to the concept of perceptual space in general, which does underlie all the so-called "plastic arts," and which serve to make them one family. Each member has its own way of being; we need not be afraid to miss the basic relationship by recognizing such separate ways. The primary illusion is not the scene—that is only one articulation of it—but of *virtual space*, however constructed.[31]

So, in contrast to the traditional assumption, theatre is heterogeneously "enactment in *virtual space*." Arena demands a different sort of articulation.

If arena, like sculpture, is three-dimensional, then in what sense can it be said to create space for the eye? The question itself may suggest why so many persist in dealing with arena as though it were still "scene," just as Hildebrand thought of sculpture as a "many-sided picture." Ultimately this kind of approach reduces images (made in round space) to mere two-dimensional semblances.

Three-dimensional space is clearly not appropriate to create "scene." Although she was speaking about sculpture when she made these remarks, Langer's idea applies to theatre when she points out that three dimensional space is suitable for "... *volume*. The volume, however, is not cubic measure, like the space in a box. It is more than the bulk of a figure; it is space made visible, and it is more than the area which the figure actually occupies."[32] To an inspiring extent, Langer's propositions about sculpture seem quite assimilable to the conditions of arena's three-dimensional stage. It is provocative and rewarding to track them further.

Langer invites speculation about the source of an illusion created in *volume*:

> The source of this illusion (for empty space, un-
> enclosed, has actually no visible parts or shape) is the fun-
> damental principle of sculptural volume: the semblance of
> organisms. In the literature of sculpture, more than any-
> where else, one meets with references to "inevitable form,"
> "necessary form," and "inviolable form." But what do these
> expressions mean? What, in nature, makes forms "inevi-
> table," "necessary," "inviolable"? Nothing but *vital function*.
> Living organisms maintain themselves, resist change, strive
> to restore their structure when they have been forceably
> interfered with. All other patterns are kaleidoscopic and
> casual; but organisms, performing characteristic func-
> tions, must have certain forms, or perish.[33]

Those terms are potent and evocative for us to consider as we attempt to pin-down the source of arena's illusion. The roots of sculptural form which Langer identifies have a comparable application to arena theatre; namely, a semblance of *vital function*. Drama is built around a psychological infrastructure which gives nascence to its conflicts and crises; for all intents and purposes these reflect a kind of organic vital structure. These appear to correspond to the principle Langer has just outlined. If drama may be perceived as such a semblance of living organisms, then it clearly follows that the actions of its characters can be described as efforts to "maintain, resist, or strive to restore their organic or psychological well-being."

This hypothesis, then, that arena theatre also deals with *vital function* may earn substantial credibility from an often-detected phenomenon. Time and again reasonably sensitive actors report during the process of rehearsing plays on arena stages an urgent need to play a scene, or maybe some section of a speech, at some specific location on the stage. They seem compelled by a concern for the psychological truth or rightness of the moment. But arena stages are devoid of histrionic platforms. There are no artificial devices whereby an actor, by dint of his location, could "take focus"—that is, absorb audience attention to himself, and away from other actors, simply as a result of his stage position. It is not merely a matter of "upstaging." More likely than not, the actor is giving stage rather than assuming it. What is noteworthy is not that actors volunteer their ideas; rather, the issue is what they evidently *feel*. Because of the nature of arena stages, it is probable that the actors become readily attuned to psychological *vital function*. It prompts them to intuit a form for action which is "inevitable," "necessary," and "inviolable." Thus Langer's comment about sculpture is equally true about arena: "No other kind of form is actually necessary. . . . Only life, once put in motion, achieves certain forms inevitably, so long as it goes on at all."[34]

Importantly, nothing is "actually alive" about this organic form (either in sculpture or in an arena play). For, even though "live" actors are employed, they aren't actually "living their roles." Ted Shank buries that idea:

> Of all artists, the actor is most often thought to express actual feelings in a symptomatic way. It is generally assumed that while on stage he takes on the feelings of the character he is acting and "becomes the character." There are several reasons that actual feelings are more frequently attributed to actors then to other dramatic artists. Like the playwright, director, and designer, the actor has a creative mind, but unlike them his own body and voice serve as his principal materials. When the actor as creative artist is separated from the materials he uses, as in a work using puppets, there is no longer such a strong tendency to assume that the apparent emotions of the character are experienced as actual emotions by the artist—the puppet operator—and of course, no one suggests that the puppet actually experiences these emotions.[35]

Nothing in an arena play is any more *actually* organic than would be anything in a piece of marble sculpture. Langer declares:

> Only its form is the form of life, and the space it makes visible is vitalized as it would be by organic activity at its center. It is *virtual kinetic volume*, created by—and with—the semblance of living form.[36]

The major premise here, then, is that the fictional world of a play is, after all, non-organic; yet its form has the semblance of living form. The space made visible through portrayal of a fictional world on an arena stage is vitalized (to borrow an expression) as a result of the fictional psychological activity at the core of such a drama. Because each uses three-dimensional space, both arena theatre and sculpture create semblances which become articulated in *virtual kinetic volume*. Langer endeavors to describe the different mode of audience perception required for "round space" as distinct from that of "scene":

> Here we have the primary illusion, virtual space, cre-
> ated in a mode quite different from that of painting, which
> is *scene*, the field of direct vision. Sculpture creates an
> equally visible space, but not the space of direct vision; for
> volume is really given originally to touch, both haptic
> touch and contact limiting bodily movement, and the
> business of sculpture is to translate its data into entirely
> visual terms, i.e., *to make tactual space visible.*[37]

Is there a point to making "tactual space visible" in the drama?
Additionally, how can this help to enlighten man in regard to his own
human condition? How can it acquaint him with new knowledge that
other sorts of theatre have failed to provide? Such questions stimulate
artistic imaginations, entice and stir the creativity of writers, and
excite other artists of the theatre. Parallels with sculpture yield
pertinent ideas for a study of arena, but how does sculpture help
organize man's perceptions? Langer responds:

> Sculptural form is a powerful abstraction from actual
> objects and the three-dimensional space which we con-
> strue by means of them, through touch and sight. It makes
> its own construction in three dimensions, namely the *sem-
> blance* of kinetic space. Just as the field of one's direct vision
> is organized, in actuality, as a plane at a distance of a
> natural focus, so the kinetic realm of tangible volumes, or
> things, and free air space between them, is organized in
> each person's actual experience as his *environment*, i.e., a
> space whereof he is the center; his body and the range of its
> free motion, its breathing space and the reach of its limbs,
> are his own kinetic volume, the point of orientation from
> which he plots the world of tangible reality—objects, dis-
> tances, motions, shape and size and mass.[38]

In the twentieth century all art seems to have come to reflect man in the
center of tangible reality. Modern drama, like all modern artistic
endeavor, can be characterized as ego-centered. The emergence and
blossoming of arena theatre seems to be a spontaneous and quite
natural intuitive response to the new conditions man finds in his
world in this era. According to Aristotle, man has always needed to
express his experience, the better to cope with it.

Now, however, mankind has entered the space age. The
system of Italianate perspective no longer organizes reality in a way
which helps man to plot or to comprehend his "space" within the social
or universal matrix. Man in only two dimensions is no modern. Two-
dimensional man is a quaint relic of the past, of a hierarchal view of the

human condition. Today, man is asserting a freedom that transcends the ephemeral world of hierarchies and politics and seeks to traverse inner and outer space, indeed which seeks to explore the limits of his universe, be it galactical and too far away to see through telescopes or molecular and too small to see through the most powerful microscopes. Modern man has come to understand that he is indeed, as John Paul Sartre expressed it in *Les Mouches*, "a mite in the scheme of things." But far from being purely existential in his attitude, man continually seeks spiritual causes and effects, searches for new worlds to explore and conquer, often seeks a justification for his existence in his relationship to his universe rather than solely in his abstract being and his isolation from it. In doing so, he pushes the frontiers of his space ever outward. The theatre can help man organize his experiences of what is, in fact, a new reality—to relate him to spatial environment in which his only orientation is his own center.

In arena theatre a semblance of man virtually organizing his way through the ebb and flow of psychological and philosophical exprience may be depicted. Arena offers "the image of man's destiny enacted in the kinetic volume of sensory space." When an audience attends a play staged in arena, it does not, of course, identify the play's space as its own space, personally and individually, any more that it would treat the space centered in a sculpture as its own space. The two are objectively perceived. They become images of the perceptor's space:

> Though a statue is, actually, an object, we do not treat
> it as such; we see it as a center of a space all its own; but its
> kinetic volume and the environment it creates are illu-
> sory—and they exist for our vision alone, a semblance of
> the self and its world.[39]

The arena play also exists for our vision (and our ears); however, it is not for vision in the mode of "scene." It is a vision of the tactual, kinetic world. The actual objects, stage, actors, movement, the audience, are not what attract attention: rather the focus is on the image which presents a concept of our own surrounding space. The precise purpose of the arena medium is to create and present such images of man in his kinetic environment. This is the reason the differences between pictorial space and round space must be carefully discerned.

Modern arena theatre has labored through a series of misrepresentations of this crucial difference. For instance, in the 1950's when arena was in the full throes of its novel popularity, a spate of books purported to explain its qualities, but hedged their enthusiasms. *Flexibility* was to be more their *cause celébre.* The complaint that arena was "too rigid" an arrangement simply cheated a careful discernment of its real nature. Usually such equivocating left the artist with no unique appreciation of the aesthetic properties of whatever medium he would finally choose. The result has been to retard forthright adoption of arena theatre for what it can do best.

Similarly, the remarks of critic, John Gassner, were easily misconstrued if one held a faulty understanding of arena's modality. His bellwether critique of the original New York production of *Summer and Smoke* at the first Circle-in-the-Square playhouse was widely scrutinized by people seeking to further understand the arena theatre. Gassner described the production:

> Stage movement was compressed by a concentrating darkness, so that it was not action but *tension* that was most manifest in the production. The characters moved within an inner darkness, never emerging into free and sharply lit space. They seemed to belong to their inner compulsions rather than to an environment beyond and independent of them.[40]

A superficial reading of Gassner's statements may lead one to a conclusion which is diametrically untrue. Gassner appears to be endorsing characters who do not relate to their *environment.* Hence, one could presume he is implying that arena should not traffic with *environment.* But a more careful observation reveals that Gassner speaks of an environment which is "beyond and independent of" the characters. What he means is "scene." By Langer's definition of environment it is a contradiction in terms to speak of an *environment* which is independent of the characters. It is actually meaningless to talk of an *environment* as being something apart from the mind which interprets. The environment of a room exists only through the *perception* of those who enter it. Different people will have an altogether different perception, individually, and based on each person's own experience, education, background, philosophy, etc. Furthermore, the crepuscular atmosphere which Gassner attributes to the production otherwise seems as neat a description of a "psychological environment" as one could hope to envision. Hence, arena's concern, like that of sculpture, is with creating *environment* not *scene.* Vigilance is demanded in order to avoid forfeiting the very essence of the medium.

Implications from the motive arts

Although significant comparisons can be made between theatre and sculpture, particularly between arena staging and sculpted art, sculpture is, of course, static, whereas theatre is dynamic. Indeed, attempts to approximate sculpture in theatre has a name: *tableau*. While sculpture can flow and be said to have "movement" in an aesthetic sense, it does not create an image in the mode of experiential time, only in the mode of experiential space. In other words, it captures and freezes images—often images in motion, but the important point is that they are frozen by the sculpture itself.

Drama, by its very nature, creates images in both time and space by using the human figure in motion. Indeed, the aesthetic principles of arena theatre are profoundly affected by the time mode, and it is most visibly articulated for us through motion.

All drama is thought to have evolved from Greek festive dances. It is surely not coincidence that such dances were performed in circles, and for that fact are physically related to the modern arena.[41] These "Reigen," as they were called, actually were primitive religious rites. For that reason one finds a degree of metaphysical conjecture about the possible religious implications inherent in the round form. Is the circular or round form an intrinsically ritualistic form? Is it somehow a "magic circle"? Such questions encourage attention to the potential relevance of the circular form as applied to modern theatre.

In order to fully appreciate and understand the implications behind the term "kinetic volume" (literally: volume pertaining to motion), it is necessary to reflect upon the very different kind of illusion created by dance. The means whereby dance creates its art is similar if not identical to the same means whereby "kinetic volume" is articulated in arena theatre. Langer offers a glimpse into the formation in the art of dance:

> Gesture is the basic abstraction whereby dance illusion is made and organized.
>
> Gesture is vital movement; to one who performs it, it is known very precisely as a kinetic experience, i.e., as action, and somewhat more vaguely by sight, as an effect. To others it appears as a visible motion, but not a motion of things, sliding, or waving, or rolling around—it is *seen and understood* as vital movement. So it is at once subjective and objective, personal and public, willed (or evoked) and perceived.[42]

As the term is employed here, *gesture* applies to the entire motor response from the first stimulus to the completed action and not merely to a small movement, a narrower meaning of the term. While Langer observes that gesture is the means through which dance creates its illusion, she further notes that it is at once a *signal*, in the sense that it is an actual motion, and *symbolic*, because it also conveys to the percipient an idea or concept of human feeling.

In motion arts it is not only people running or moving around which we see; we also see a relationship between the figures—a relationship of vital forces is conveyed. Such figures seem to attract and repel, like magnets. A virtual sense of energy, active or potential, seems to pervade. Langer states: "The primary illusion of dance is a virtual realm of Power—not actual, physically exerted power, but the appearances of influence and agency created by virtual gesture."[43]

The important concept here is how the dance uses space, how it creates the appearance of powers acting upon the performer, how it magnetizes and gives symbolic meaning to its space. Such information has direct influence over the way arena space can be articulated. Dance images are created from an idea of vital consciousness, wherein the dancer awakens to his own internal vital force, and to those external forces which play upon him. Langer elaborates:

> The prototype of the purely apparent energies is not the "field of forces" known to physics, but the subjective experience of volition and free agency, and of reluctance to alien, compelling wills. The consciousness of life, the sense of vital power, even the power to receive impressions, apprehend the environment, and meet changes, is our most immediate self-consciousness. This is the feeling of power; and the play of such "felt" energies is as different from any system of physical forces as psychological time is from clock time, and psychological space from the space of geometry.[44]

Just as drama may be described as a semblance of living organisms striving to achieve well-being, it can be further refined as being an interplay of characters swayed by psychological powers of volition in combat with the powers of destiny. One can immediately begin to envision a commanding form for a play from this concept, just as well as one might see from it a theme for a dance. Langer identifies such clashes of vital energies as those "wherein purely imaginal beings from whom the vital force emanates shape a world of dynamic forms by their magnet-like, psycho-physical action."[45]

George Bernard Shaw's "Arms And The Man," Kalamazoo [Michigan] Civic Players

"Candide," by Bernstein, 1980, California State University, Long Beach

Setting for "The Gingerbread Lady," Kalamazoo [Michigan] Civic Players

Insofar as aesthetic principles may govern the criteria, there were no true arena theatres before this century. Arena is a product of the needs of expression of our age. Historians allege that the circular form is ages old, but their presumption must fall of its own weight, on grounds that the *aesthetic principles of round space* never operated in their pre-twentieth century examples. To the contrary, the overriding principles operating behind their examples were essentially derived from ideas of *scenic* space. What is astonishing, because it so clearly parallels our own contentions about the Greek actors, is Mrs. Langer's analysis of the evolution of dance, itself. Her distinctions between dance intended to be worship and dance meant to enthrall audiences are of critical importance for what they tell us. While her explanation is quite lengthy, it is striking for the implications that can be drawn regarding arena theatre. She says:

> A new demand is made on the dance when it is to enthrall not only its own performers, but a passive audience (rustic audiences that furnish the music by singing and clapping are really participants; they are not included here). The dance as a spectacle is generally regarded as a product of degeneration, a secularized form of what is really a religious art. But it is really a natural development even within the confines of the "mythic consciousness," for dance magic may be projected to a spectator, to cure, purify, or initiate him. Tyler describes a savage initiation ceremony in which boys solemnly witnessed a dog dance performed by older men. Shamen, medicine men, witch doctors and magicians commonly perform dances for their magical effects, not upon the dancer, but on the awed spectators.
>
> From the artistic standpoint this use of the dance is a great advance over the purely ecstatic, because addressed to an audience the dance becomes essentially and not only incidentally a spectacle, and thus finds its true creative aim—to make the world of powers visible. This aim dictates all sorts of new techniques because bodily experiences, muscular tensions, momentum, the feeling of precarious balance or the impulsions of imbalance, can no longer be counted on to give form or continuity to the dance. Every such kinesthetic element must be replaced by visual, audible, or histrionic elements to create a comparable ecstatic illusion for the audience. At this stage the problems of the tribal or cult dance are practically those of the modern ballet: to break the beholder's sense of actuality and set up the virtual image of a different world; to create a play of forces that *confronts* the percipient, instead of

> engulfing him, as it does when he is dancing, and his own
> activity is a major factor in making the dance illusion.
>   The presence of an audience gives the dance its artistic
> discipline; for instance where the dancers perform to royal
> spectators, choreographic art soon becomes a highly con-
> scious, formalized, and expert presentation . . .[46]

Those circular forms of dance known as the "Reigen"—highly-charged, potent, eerily awesome—when taken in the context of ritual power negotiations, are presumed, by Mrs. Langer's accounts, characteristically to *engulf* their audiences. Due to their irresistible rhythms and vibrating activity, they constantly threaten to sweep nearby passive viewers up into their ecstacy. The obvious alternative which was somehow deemed the only conceivable way to ward off such engulfment became to separate the performer from the audience, affording a situation of "confrontation." This is just another way of saying that an audience is distanced from actuality when one establishes between the performer and the beholder a *presentational axis*. The emotional intensity which overflows from such circle dances must be appreciated to understand why, among such primitive peoples, no choice of a middle-ground was even considered; for the viewer the only possibilities seemed to be *engulfment*, or else the more contemplative status of *confrontation*. Anthropological film studies by Margaret Mead of certain Balinese circle dances help to convey even in modern times some notion of how totally consuming this orgiastic, ecstatic spell could be.

Augusto Boal, the self-proclaimed Marxist founder of the Arena Theatre of Sao Paulo, Brazil, offers an unusual explanation for the historical withdrawal of spectators from the thrall of ritual dance in his book, *Theatre of the Oppressed*. Boal declares such a withdrawal represented the beginning of oppression by the ruling classes over the proletariat. He says:

> The ruling classes took possession of the theater and
> built their dividing walls. First they divided the people,
> separating actors from spectators: people who act and
> people who watch—the party is over! Secondly, among
> the actors, they separated the protagonist from the mass.
> The coercive indoctrination began![47]

Señor Boal's radical reading of history is incidental to a more important fact. With keen insight, Boal has clearly apprehended that transactions of power are inherent to the circular form. Whether disengaging spectators from performers was due to a purported power-grab by a "ruling-class," or was merely a natural devolution whose effect was never presupposed, is of far less consequence to arena theatres than is clearly understanding, as Boal does, arenas articulate *power negotiations*. Greek dramatic theatre, however, because its spectators were ultimately disengaged from its performers, could no longer articulate such *negotiations of power*.

Mrs. Langer has chronicled the beginnings of drama in this fashion:

> The fact that Greek drama arose amidst ritual dancing has led several art historians to consider it as a dance episode; but dance was, in fact, only a perfect framework for the development of an entirely new art; the minute the two antagonists stepped out of the choric ensemble and addressed not the diety, nor the congregation, but each other, they created the poetic illusion, and drama was born in the midst of religious rite.[48]

Prior to the twentieth century no one had challenged the shibboleth, either *engulfment or confrontment*. Indeed, stage directors (or their surrogates) were the only likely figures to test its validity, and before the mid-nineteenth century, the role of stage director was only rarely assigned to a differentiated artist. When artistic experiments such as various directors would employ as a matter of course in the modern theatre became a commonplace, they revealed that the "world of powers" could only be made visible through motion in space. But, importantly, no law of nature mandates that a spectator must face or confront such an illusory world in order for it to become visible to him. Indeed, he may perfectly "see" such a world in a similar way as he may recognize the illusory world of the sculpture. That is, he may envision it through a reckoning within his own mind.

Inextricably, arena evokes in people's minds both challenges and power negotiations. Arena is universally conceived to be a dynamic, potentially volatile medium precisely because it courts that capacity to engulf. Yet theatre arts emphatically exist to create *illusions*, not actualities; they attempt to present *concepts* of human feeling, not to induce actual human feeling. Augusto Boal's theory for arena theatre (while it may well fascinate many people), would pre-meditatedly banish this all-crucial precept of illusion for theatre arts. Boal's concern, like many before him—dictators, revolutionaries, political activists, and even evangelists—is to coopt theatre to serve as an instrument of propaganda and deliberate incitement. Boal's idea of arena staging explicitly sets out to eradicate the role of spectator, to intentionally *engulf* his theatre-goers, and to egg them toward incipient revolution. In ironic contrast with Boal's theory, however, remains the fact that two world-renowned Soviet directors, Nikolai Okhlopkov and Boris Zakhava, giants of the early arena theatre movement, received hasty ends to both their careers and lives, precisely because their arena productions threatened to *engulf* and stir up their Moscow audiences. Unquestionably, when illusion disappears and the perception of feelings is replaced by the actual feelings themselves, then the activity at hand departs the realm of art, and simply becomes real life.

"Confronting" an illusory world *a l'Italien* seems essentially contradictory to twentieth-century man's system of plotting and coping with space from his own center. It is contrary to his perceived expectations of reality in the more-democratically organized world in which he lives, or at least to which he subscribes. Out of man's evolving realizations was born a new concept, motion-in-the-round, which dismisses the non-democratic, hierarchical contrivance of pictorial organization in favor of concentrating on that essential interplay of Powers. It presents an image to man which is like the way he grapples with the Powers and forces in his own life.

The chief advantages of arena theatre are to be found in arena's new focus, a concentrated, in-depth focus on dramatic interplay. This amounts to a new way, to be sure, of apprehending the concept. It is not an ocular but a mental focus. The most appropriate way to describe it may be to define it as the *dramatic event*, which is the contrary of the dramatic spectacle. Here again, the properties of *environment* versus *scene* become important. In a book written nearly seventy years ago and entitled *Reference Point*, Arthur Hopkins, a Broadway director, states:

> Actors must play to each other—not the audience. . . .
> The purpose of the *circular* concept is to make the play a
> self-contained entity, not living because of, or for, an
> audience. The play is not taken to the audience. The
> audience is to be drawn into the play.[49] [italics added]

Hopkins seems to offer a ready prescription for the realistic *cum* naturalistic *cum* representationalistic approach to the theatre. But that would be far too narrow an interpretation to attach to Hopkins' point. In a large sense he is advocating the spirit of the dramatic event, as distinguished from the blandishments of sheer spectacle. Hopkins'

advice would figuratively apply to even the most theatrical play as
much as to the most naturalistic. He is neither denying the existence
of the spectator, nor relegating him to the vantage of the peep-hole.
Rather he is charging those who would heed him with the responsibility to create a dramatic event, symbolic of human feeling.

Much has been written implying that an audience is the *sine qua
non* of drama, perhaps to compensate for the abusive, but long-held,
perception that drama was literature which was occasionally enacted.
Martin Esslin, in *An Anatomy of Drama*, asserts: "The author and the
performer are only half of the total process: the other half is the
audience and its reaction. Without an audience there is no drama."[50]

There can be no question that audience reaction, particularly
laughter, feeds back into the live performance, and alters it in percep-
tible ways. Theodore Shank offers a rationale for the input of audiences in this far more prescient explanation:

> The form of any art which exists in time is incomplete
> until the work has been perceived to the end; thus while it
> is in progress it establishes a kind of expectation which the
> percipient wants to be fulfilled. This is somewhat like the
> expectation developed in a song as one waits for the end of
> the musical phrase and the rhyme. Accompanying this
> suspense of form in dramatic art there is frequently a sus-
> pense of plot; an unanswered question to which the audi-
> ence wants an answer . . .[51]

Yet nothing in either of these writer's remarks would fundamentally contradict Hopkins' intial point which reasoned that the
circular play is a dramatic event into whose consequences an audience
should be drawn. It is not mere gratuitous spectacle presented to
amuse them with frivolous or temporary stimulation. If theatre is to
be meaningful it must by *symbolic*, which enriches it cognitively to a
deeper level than mere ecstatic orgies or vicarious emotional thrills.

Arenas have always been sites of momentous struggles, often
between powers of life and death. How is it, for instance, that surgical
training is invariably conducted for medical students in operating
arenas? The *event* transpiring on a surgical table poses all the clinical
truth one could ever hope to witness. A false move has observable,
perhaps disastrous, consequences. Likewise consider how the highwire
act in a circus arena acquires an absorption so intense that spectators
can hardly control their own breath. Even the arenas of sporting
events virtually impel one to anticipate the showdown: who will win,
lose or draw? These, as well as cock fights, duels, executions, are *real*

actions, and the arena form favors actions that are *done*, not merely *shown*. Showing involves the audience-axis. Arenas are life's theatres of momentous events. Events of public consequence, great transactions of power, are played out to their final resolution in the arena forum.

SECTION THREE: Assembling a Working Theory

Susanne Langer challenges the theatre artist "to produce and sustain the illusion. . . ."[52] The fundamental and, perhaps, most important element of illusion-making begins with the playwright who generally conceives the "fiction" of the play itself. Sometimes improvisation or extemporaneous theatre by-pass the need for formal playwriting—yet there must always be the construction of a fictitious event by one means or another. Such storytelling establishes what Langer labels "the poetic illusion." About this she remarks: "The dramatic illusion is poetic, and where it is primary—that is to say, where the work is a drama—it transmutes all borrowings from other arts into poetic elements."[53]

The commanding form of an enacted drama is established in its initial conception by the artistic imagination of the playwright. To a large degree he becomes the first architect of the work. But the precise mixture of drama's component contributions can often be misunderstood. Hence, Langer clarifies:

> Once we recognize that drama is neither dance nor literature, nor a democracy of various arts functioning together, but is poetry in the mode of action, the relations of all its elements to each other and to the whole work become clear: the primacy of the script, which furnishes the commanding form; the use of the stage, with or without representational scenery, to delimit a "world" in which the virtual action exists . . .[54]

No matter what other illusions are borrowed, as for example those of sculptural space and dance, no matter which theatre media are ultimately employed, arena or some other, the goal is always singular: the articulation of the poetic illusion, which is drama. To a very great extent, of course, this is a combined effort. The technical

support for any production ranging from lights to makeup to costumes is no less important than the actors' talents and the directors'
visions in translating the playwright's imagination from printed word
to motion and the fulfillment of a stage's space. Eric Bently, arguably
the most influential theatre critic in the United States, declares: "All
theatre 'arts' are means to one end: the correct presentation of a
poem."[55] The performance of drama in arena initiates its illusion from
the work of the playwright, along the way integrating the work of all
artisans and the secondary illusions they create, into its "apparition of
Destiny."

The boundaries of illusion

Often artists of the theatre hold a seriously misplaced notion of
the mission of art in the world. Instead of simply portraying as
truthful an image of human feeling as they can, they are overcome by
a sense of mission to reform society or the world. Impatient with
illusion—in fact, unconvinced that mere theatre can have any true
relevance in the real world—they labor to obscure the distinction
between life and art, illusion and actuality. What is sometimes lost or
obscured is the recognition that theatre, under whatever pretext it is
presented, is always from beginning to end an *illusion*. Reduced to its
simplest, however, the fact remains: theatre, like any other art, is
completely illusion.

Consequently, to begin examining how artists might articulate
a work for arena, one should first consider how to establish the bounds
of its illusory world. Quite obviously, for the sorts of material just
described, the question has rather been: how to *blur* those boundaries
of the illusory world, so that the play apparently becomes part of the
percipient's actual life. Audiences by now have become inured to such
incursions into their privacy. They no longer react with resentment,
irritation, or fear, but are merely blasé toward such pandering. The
times seem finally to be demanding a return to honest and more-
profound illusion-making.

The two most frequently used methods for establishing the
limits of the illusory world in the overwhelming majority of arena
playhouses are by controlled lighting and by sound. There is no
reason why these two always ought to be the means for setting the
fictional world "off from the surrounding world of actuality"; nor, in-

deed, are they always so employed. Outdoor daylight performances would gain little discernible illumination from theatrical lighting. In such circumstances, therefore, lights would be of little use to mark a separation of actuality from fiction.

Nevertheless, the lowering of houselights in most indoor theatres signals the spectators that the play is about to begin. A nearly subconscious (reflexive) mental-focal adjustment is made by such audiences, preparing them to pay attention, not merely as various individuals functioning separately, but also gradually bonding together as a sort of cohesive psychological entity. As the stage lights rise the audience more and more ceases to resist the sway of the illusory world.

Often this transition from the harsh real world to the fictional world of the play is facilitated by the use of sound or music, either live or recorded. This tends to heighten the theatrical anticipation of an audience because an aural illusion is already penetrating one of their major senses, and crowding out external distractions.

Although these methods have become practically traditional as arena theatre conventions, there are still other possibilities; it is up to the imagination of artistic talents to regard the establishment of illusory worlds as one of their more important creative challenges.

Symbolic applications of light and sound

Light and sound serve as *signals* which separate the illusory world from the real. However, they also have a *symbolic* function in the arena that goes beyond their normal value to traditional theatre forms.

Stage lighting, besides illuminating the fictional territory of the play, also functions as a profoundly expressive tool. As Adolph Appia detailed over ninety years ago, by color, tone, intensity, shadow, shape, and nowadays, even movement, lighting helps to mold the visual perception of objects on the stage, while concurrently it can even change altogether the very image audiences perceive, either as a gradual matter or abruptly. Hence, lighting can be said to "act" in creating the final form of the work. In this way it assists in articulating the ultimate *symbolic* meaning of the enacted play.

Sound, as well, can function as an integral component of the work's imagery. Nature, however, causes certain curious psycho-physical phenomena to occur with "sound-in-the-round." For ex-

"The Venetian Twins," 1971-2, Theatre Three, Dallas, Texas

"The Great Gesture," by Rodolfo Usigli, Tufts Arena Theatre

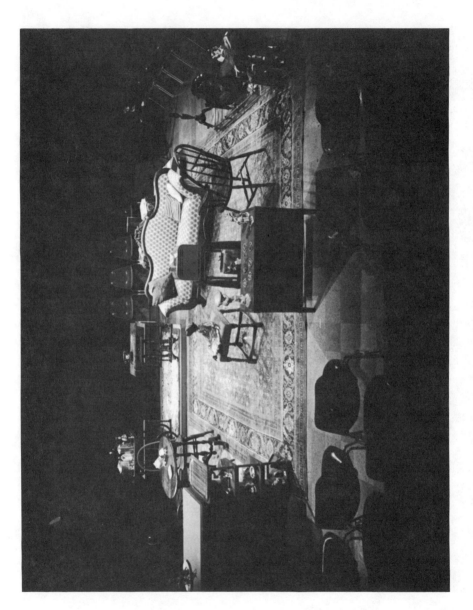

Setting, "The Killing of Sister George," Kalamazoo [Michigan] Civic Players

ample, a gunshot at close range in the arena is quite likely to jar audiences into overt reaction, dispelling all sense of illusion. To expect audiences to be able to "disbelieve" the loud noise of a gunshot is to wish for impossibilities. The sudden, penetrating, aural stimulation will almost assuredly disrupt an audience's concentration. In a manuscript describing sound uses for arena, Kelly Yeaton observes: "It cannot be overemphasized that in theater sound provides a stronger bond between audience and play than does sight, because sound is heard at nearly the same instant by audience and player alike."[56] Sound can become just "too authentic" for art; more than other elements, it can bring sometimes unpredictable results. Gunfire is only one example of how an audience's attention may be deflected to something *actual*. On one occasion the author can recall hearing recorded "cricket noises" that seemed to draw too much attention to themselves, instead of to the play. Plainly, great care and good taste are required to assure that sound effects enhance the illusory fabric woven for the play.

Ideally, since arena is primarily a theatre of environment, sound ought to provide a particularly effective vehicle for expression. Although nowadays sound is heavily employed in "scene" theatres, too, most probably it is more effectively utilized for expressive purposes in-the-round. Stereo and multi-directional sound seem obviously propitious for three-dimensional theatre.

Such sound enhancements call to mind once more the film's paradoxical efforts to "involve" spectators, particularly through 3-D photography or wrap-around screens, accompanied by high-powered stereophonic and directional-source sound. Such enterprises tend to mock and deny the very medium in which they have been constructed, and amount to little more than expensive travesties. Certainly they succeed in "involving" spectators, by getting them to respond physically to roller-coaster or bob-sled rides, or whatever. The vicarious thrill is triggered from a confused response induced inappropriately as though it were to something actual. Such efforts may be more fun-house than art. Unfortunately, that is a distinction which even arena theatres sometimes have the terrible temptation to forget.

Articulating a play in round space

Back in 1905 a prophetic Gordon Craig issued this remarkable prognostication:

> The theater of the future will be a theater of visions, not a theater of sermons nor a theater of epigrams . . . an art which says less yet shows more than all; an art which is simple for all to understand it feelingly; an art which springs from movement, movement which is the very symbol of life.[57]

Craig's oracular description nearly breathes the words: ARENA THE-ATRE. Indeed, "movement which is the very symbol of life,"— movement not fettered with artificial perspective—is precisely what artists may create in arena theatre.

Motion in arena theatre is perceived and understood because it is plotted in the same way man plots his own perception of space. Arena audiences instinctively comprehend this, not merely because of their proximity or intimacy with the performers, but precisely because throughout their daily lives they go about plotting their own surroundings virtually in an identical manner. Particularly in the context of the ebb and flow of "powers," arenas always provide optimal theatres.

To articulate a play in three-dimensional space requires setting up some meaningful plan, an over-all structure, symbolic of human feeling. Such a plan should be capable of providing the beholder an effective, sharp insight into the play's crises, and a comprehension of the "destiny" which moves inexorably toward fulfillment through the actions of the characters. Haphazard motion, or motion designed merely to afford various segments of audience a better view of actors from time to time, will not suffice, since these are void of vital symbolic structure.

Kelly Yeaton, an expert artist in arena theatre, devised two important fundamental techniques for "programming" the space of an arena stage. This sort of programming tends automatically to articulate and integrate all motion. Fortunately these techniques can be adapted to virtually every situation. He describes how they operate:

> The stage is truly an arena of dramatic conflict, in which the primary movement of the actors will be determined by the position of opponents and allies of each instant. It is also a sort of crossroads, the symbolic area of

> decision, in which the future course of action is deter-
> mined. Perhaps for this reason most arena stages use four
> opposite entrances. When the direction of each is deter-
> mined by the director an armature for action is fixed. it is
> often desirable to have the exits designated in such a
> manner that the central decisions of the play become
> definite choices of direction in the arena space.[58]

It is, however, in the application of such techniques that the real
significance emerges.

1. The interplay of forces

The first concept built into Yeaton's techniques articulates the
psycho-physical relationships between one force and another—Power
versus Power, antagonists versus protagonist. The play of forces
between these fictional characters *magnetizes* the space between them;
every move by the character actually depicts either a sort of dynamic
attraction or repulsion impelled by their "vital" wills. Each player
creates and presents a kinetic image of virtual stimulation and response. Such interplay between "vital" forces may be thought of as
resembling a bullfight: a bull charges toward a matador, who dodges,
narrowly missing calamity. The bull surges past, stops, turns, paws
the earth and prepares to attack once again. The drama continues in
this fashion. Even during those brief seconds when both adversaries
may be facing away from each other, they are both unmistakably and
instinctively aware of the force which the other represents. Similarly,
in the void of arena space, actors may actually "charge" the atmosphere with tension to the opponent symbolic force by employing this
concept. The protagonist may serve as symbol of one force; the
antagonist as symbol of a contrary force. In the words of choreogra-
pher, Arthur Michel, the audience will "realize the human being as a
tension in space. . . ."[59] This creates a dynamic, psychologically honest
axis for motion between forces. Naturally, as the opponents approach
one another the audience becomes aware of a greater "charge" in the
space between the two; anxieties abate somewhat as they move apart.
    Nature is ruled by a complex of laws. To create tension on an
arena stage also might be considered somewhat like an elastic rubber-
band which offers little resistence unless it is stretched. Hence, as in
the bullfight scenario, any lapse in concentration, any change of inter-

est, between the bull and the matador would dissipate that charged tension. Such tensions are realized as a matter of concerted will. This all works very much like simple magnetism. Two magnetic poles are inexorably attracted or repelled by one another; but introduce a third magnet, and the relationship between the original poles is altered. Moreover, if each of the poles remains too far out of range, one will not draw the other sufficiently to observe this tension. To complicate matters even further, actors can regulate the amount of magnetic push/pull they sense toward other forces, thereby varying it. At one moment the tension may be felt strongly, at another it may be scarcely felt at all, depending upon the circumstances of the scene and whether the other force seems threatening or benign.

   Figure 6 illustrates the basic interplay of forces. When one of the characters crosses laterally to a new location on the stage, the polar axis between the characters shifts right along and continues to "charge" the new relative space between them. As more and more symbolic

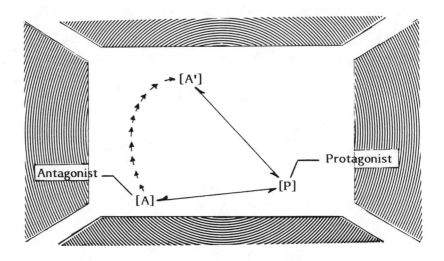

Figure 6
The interplay of forces

forces are added to the interplay, a whole network of "tension" axes emerges. On a three-dimensional stage interpersonal axes do not need to be warped into grotesque synthetic structures that are imposed for pictorialism; instead they have the full, free truth of a 360° sweep in which to flow naturally, just as mankind has in real life. Each of these myriad *tension lines* establishes its own psychologically-true dimension, rather than any forced, artificial semblance. The audience intuitively responds to such "truth." Their own experience validates it or prompts awareness of its falsity.

2. The symbolic armature

Whereas the previous concept, "the interplay of forces," naturally programs the semblance of attraction and repulsion between dramatic forces within a great, arena spatial void (which operates like a magnetic force-field), the stage space itself is still amorphous. It has not yet acquired distinctive "fictional" significance—which is to say, it is no "place." Other than to provide the stage platform to contain a dramatic conflict, it affords no means of articulating the poetic content of any particular play in question. It remains just a stage, not yet transformed into that drama's illusory universe.

The next step, putting a play into the arena, requires the *construction of a symbolic design* that should articulate the environment and the great central decisions in the play. Within the volume of arena space, all motion, up until now freewheeling, will finally be able to assume a semblance impregnated with the symbolic meanings assigned through such a spatial design.

This same design function was also necessary in "scene" theatres, though it has invariably been fulfilled by artists whose perceptions of drama are understood in visual, pictorial terms. Indeed, the French even label this planner the *metteur-en-scène* or *mise-en-scène*. Arena, however, wants a reconceptualization of this function; hereafter, this all-crucial design must be fashioned with primarily kinetic, motive images in mind. The task now actually requires a sort of *metteur-en-environnement*. The space of the stage must be mapped through a carefully oriented, symbolic plan. This affords every movement within the structure to become a visible articulation of some nuance of the play's meaning, rather than aimless, arbitrary dumb-show. Langer, who urges artists to expand upon her ideas, says:

> In the theatre, where a virtual future unfolds before us,
> the import of every little act is heightened, because even
> the smallest act is oriented toward that future. What we
> see, therefore, is not behavior, but the self-realization of
> people in action and passion; and every act has exagger-
> ated importance, so the emotional responses of a person in
> a play are intensified. Even indifference is a concentrated
> and significant attitude.[60]

The technique of a *symbolic armature* affords a method of organizing space symbolically and for assigning meaning to the space of an arena stage. Through its employment, motion will automatically relate to the meaning of the play. The selective focus of the viewers will gravitate to the momentary events holding the characters' atten-tion, rather than to some artificial emphasis inflicted through pictorial focus. The technique of a symbolic armature is as providential for the use of the arena medium as "the wash" technique is for the watercolor medium.

Kelly Yeaton inferred earlier that the four entrance aisles found in most arena theatres are no mere coincidence. More than simple architectural or economic exigency, more than an option allowing for variety, these aisles establish paths that intersect at mid-stage in an arena. Such an arrangement (portrayed in Figure 7 on page 95) has im-plications which penetrate far deeper than merely affording necessary access to the stage.

At the very minimum, the form is related to a most fundamen-tal perception of the notion of "three-dimensionality": volume, depth and breadth. This is one of the reasons so many arena theatres are so-constituted. By definition and inference, round space affords the ability to move toward all points of the compass. For one to ascend or descend, up or down in elevation, becomes another matter; those directions are influenced through gravitational laws. Even when platforms, risers, staircases, or other devices are employed to affect and provide for movement up and down, it is impossible for an actor to move onto them without relocating in one direction or another unless, of course, he is benefitted by a suspended wire or other device which gives him the appearance of "flying" or "floating" and, thus, defying ordinary natural laws. At least under conditions of earth's gravity, motion up or down implies the introduction of physical aids, i.e., stairs, elevators, even space rocketry.

All mankind lives, works, and plays in the sort of space where, in nature, one is physically free to move both in length and breadth.

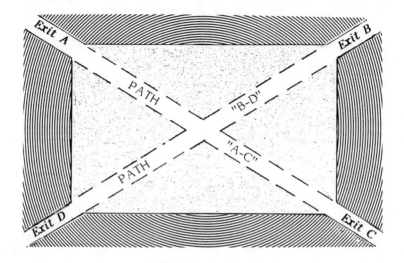

Figure 7
Arena's intersecting paths

The crossed paths of an arena stage *symbolize* that ability to extend motion in these directions. One cannot emphasize too strongly: man lives in three-dimensional space, not in flattened, pictorial space. He deals with reality in three-dimensions; intellectually, he knows the dimensions of depth to exist all around him with himself at the center of his universe. The crossed paths of an arena stage symbolize the center of the play's universe. It is a symbol of the way we acknowledge our world really to be.

> A form that is both *sign* and *symbol* ties action and insight together for us; it plays a part in a momentary situation and also in the "science" we constantly, if tacitly, assume.[61] [italics added]

Further, and for precisely the reasons Langer has just cited, the crossing paths are also an ideal symbolic form. In addition to the tacit reminder of the physical dimensions of space, there are a multitude of other qualities which make it so ideal. Langer reviews some of the stunning qualities of such symbolism. She says:

> Many symbols—not only words, but other forms— may be said to be "charged" with meanings. They have many symbolic and signific functions, and these functions have been integrated into a complex so that they are all apt to be sympathetically invoked with any chosen one. The cross is such a "charged" symbol: the actual instrument of Christ's death, hence a symbol of suffering; first laid upon his shoulders, an actual burden, as well as a product of human handiwork, and on both grounds a symbol of his accepted burden; also an ancient symbol of the four zodiac points, with a cosmic connotation; a natural symbol of *cross-roads* [italics added] (we still use it on our highways as a warning before an intersection), and therefore of decision, crisis, choice; also of *being crossed*, i.e., of frustration, adversity, fate; and finally, to the artistic eye a cross is the figure of a man. All these and many other meanings lie dormant in that simple, familiar, significant shape. No wonder it is a magical form: it is charged with meanings, all human and emotional and vaguely cosmic so that they have become integrated into a connotation of the whole religious drama—sin, suffering, and redemption. Yet undoubtedly the cross owes much of its value to the fact that *it has the physical attributes of being a good symbol*: it is easily made—drawn on paper, set up in wood or stone, fashioned of precious substance as an amulet, even traced recognizably with the finger, in a ritual gesture. It is so obvious a symbolic device that despite its holy connotations we do not refrain from using it in purely mundane, discursive capacities, as a sign of "plus," or in a tilted position as "times," or as a marker on ballot sheets and many other kinds of records.[62]

Suffering, burden, cosmic implications, decision, crises, choice, frustration, adversity, fate, and man—these are surely the substance of drama; to employ the form which symbolizes these meanings attaches those very connotations upon the use of four aisles, a situation which one finds in nearly all arena theatres. A depth of symbolism is evoked of which most percipients never become acutely conscious. Yet such magnificent levels of symbolic expression lie ready for arena artists to penetrate and to exploit.

By rendering a design of a "symbolic armature" to a play, this second technique can be clearly illustrated. Such an illustration immediately indicates how every motion becomes articulated with meaning. The following example, though deliberately elementary, easily facilitates a comprehension of an armature.

In John Millington Synge's Irish folk-play, *The Well of the Saints*,[63] together, an old, blind husband and wife roam falteringly through the countryside of that land, each longing for the gift of sight. Presently they happen upon a holy-man who overhears their wish. He leads them to "the Well of the Saints" where a miracle occurs that restores their sight. At first the couple cannot recognize each other, and see one another only as strange, buzzardly old-crones; they hasten to part company. In time, each learns that life among the "seeing" is not exactly the paradise he or she had always imagined, so each returns to seek out the holy-man. At their request he undoes the miracle to render them both blind again, so that they may go more happily down the road of life. The great central question of this play hinges on whether the couple will ever *reunite* (on a path that is labelled "To-gether, blind," though it might finally be called: "Blind, but happy"). They eventually do so. However, the alternative to this critical decision would be to each separate onto other paths (which shall connote "Miserable, but sighted"). To create an armature which would articulate the movement of this play for an arena, one needs to assign symbolic directions to each path. Figure 8 diagrams such a symbolic construct. Each path represents a choice to the characters. Path [A] represents going to the well, where they first journey to get sight, and later return to be rid of their unwanted "gift." Path [B] represents the direction for the old man to retreat once his sight is restored, but he can no longer abide to look upon his wife. Path [C] is the direction of flight the old woman takes to escape the repugnant features of her aged husband. Path [D] represents the road they use to enter and leave together as blind people.

The action of the play is cyclical; hence, it affords a clear pattern. The couple enter from the "Together, blind" path, and once the action of the play swings full cycle, first to the Well to achieve their wish, then both going off in separate, opposed directions as a result of their unforeseen disenthrallment, only to return and revisit the Well; they finally retreat down the road from whence they first entered. The cycle has been completed, the "destined" action has been fulfilled, and the central choices of the play have been articulated.

The point of this example is how a move in any direction within

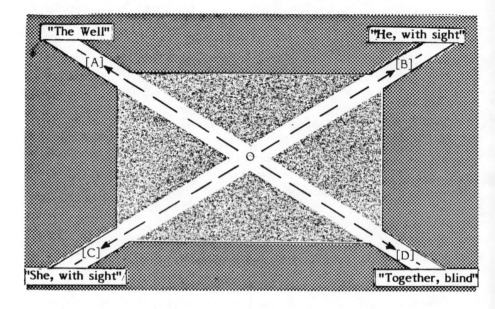

Figure 8
A symbolic armature

this structure must automatically demonstrate some meaningful choice
or decision by the character, however tentative or like a "testing-of-
the-water" such a move might be. One can understand right away that
it would be psychologically "out of character" for the man to cross
toward Path [C], the direction of "She, with sight," unless such a move
intended to goad, to taunt, or to thwart the old woman's clear retreat.
What is more, her body language would "inevitably" express her
psychological relationship toward the Path and direction of his claim
[B]. Such space orientation, developed from the poetic illusion that is
composed by the playwright, endows all movement with *inevitable*,
life-resembling patterns, motivated and rooted in psychological truth,

and not unlike the "inevitable," "necessary," and "inviolable" forms regarding dance and sculpture. These schematic patterns may strike one as no less arbitrary than the conventionalized values of a proscenium theater. However, they are not distorted for pictorial artificiality.

The crossroads is not the only symbolic form that could be constructed in the arena. *Le Théâtre en Rond* in Paris has a circular stage with only three aisles. The aisles form a "Y" set of paths onto its acting area. Here, also, one may attach to this form all of the subliminal connotations that the "Y" pattern might endow. An exactly circular stage, however, often suggests an almost too regular, perfect, or static semblance. All actors' positions tend to remain equi-distant, consequently limiting all the actor's stage-crossing to a somewhat monotonous sameness. Certainly, France's theatre delights in a symbolic expression of such balance, reason, and composure, almost in the manner of an intellectual swordsmanship match. This has been notable at least since the days of neo-classicism. Theatre of motion and action is more a trait of English language, and particularly American, theatre. Curiously, at *Le Théâtre en Rond*, one example stands out— *Ouragan sur le Caine,* an approximate translation of the American *Caine Mutiny Court Martial.* The entire play is, of course, a court trial which is essentially sedentary, hortatory, and requires very little overt action. What movement occurred in that production seemed to do little more than divert one's eye from time to time. Primarily, the concentration focused upon the intellectual contest and the language.

Nevertheless, the symbolic armature which is based upon a "Y" formation of paths remains quite a legitimate alternative to the crossing-paths. Rather than a crossroads, the stage becomes a veritable "fork in the roads." Obviously implicit within this form is the notion of *choice. The Wizard of Oz* rushes immediately to mind as an example, wherein the central question is always: Which path leads to the Emerald City? The fork in the road concept often seems to carry the baggage of moral choice, right or wrong, good or bad, correct or incorrect. Ethical selection would seem to naturally benefit from the use of this kind of armature. There are undoubtedly other potential connotations to the "Y" form. And there are still other potential symbolic arrangements. A two-aisle form which merely opens up in the center of the arena stage to provide a sort of "way-station" is yet another possible structure for articulating arena's space. The ultimate establishment of a symbolic armature is limited only by the intelligence and imagination of the arena artist. Such articulation of arena's space remains the acid test of an arena artist's skill and genius.

3. Fulfilling the play's universe

Bodily responsiveness to those symbolic ideas ascribed for each entry path becomes the means through which actors begin to articulate space on an arena stage. That responsiveness is always seen as *gesture*, whether it be as miniscule as the reflex of an eye to a sensed stimulus, or as overt a sequence of movement as the fully executed dance routine. Every "gesture" begins with the body's perceptors— the eyes, ears, nose, taste buds, skin, etc. The mind's eye processes those perceptions into imagery, and thence into physical response.

Plainly, an actor's behavior is a response to the images his character senses. Julius Fast in his study, *Body Language*, says: "Of all parts of the human body that are used to transmit information, the eyes are the most important and can transmit the most subtle nuances."[64] That which the actor imagines is that to which he reacts. If each actor can draw cognition from every entrance path, he may also imagine what those mean to his character. But what is more, the full 360° arc which encompasses the stage represents an entire fictional universe of stimuli to the actor. The world should not cease to exist between the entrance aisles. Hence, the actor must see and sense what the character would see and sense in that circumference.

Thus, the arena actor will be reactive to a series of push/pull (attraction/repulsion) stimuli from: a) the other players, b) the symbolic entrance armature, and now c), the imaginal world of the fiction—those other points of stimuli which the story demands. Such a set of stimuli may perhaps emanate from the off-stage periphery, quite far away upon a distant horizon, for example, or may even seem to arise from much closer to the stage out in the midst of where, otherwise, the audience actually is seated. One of the preeminent dangers, certainly, of allowing actors to spot-focus their eyes upon a supposed stimulus located somewhere in the midst of the audience is the likelihood that such an actor, rather than recognizing the imaginary source of that stimulus to his character (for instance, a reverie of a pastoral scene his character may be recalling) may, in fact, accidentally catch and hold the eye of someone in the audience watching his performance. The resulting embarrassment this produces springs from deep cultural roots which are nicely examined in Fast's book. "To stare is to dehumanize," Fast tells us.[65] Stares are reserved only for *non-persons*—slaves, servants, waiters, children, animals in a zoo, sideshow freaks, actors, or those of inferior positions. Fast counsels that we may use:

> . . . the stare for the side-show freak, but we do not
> really consider him a human being. He is an object at which
> we have paid money to stare, and in the same way we may
> stare at an actor on a stage. The real man is masked too
> deeply behind his role for our stare to bother either him or
> us. However, the new theater that brings the actor down
> into the audience often gives us an uncomfortable feeling.
> By virtue of involving us, the audience, the actor suddenly
> loses his non-person status and staring at him becomes
> embarrassing to us.[66]

What Fast observes here amounts to a breach of an accepted
cultural norm. Among human beings who are strangers, we custom-
arily deal with one another by implicitly offering a rapid glance of
recognition, only to be followed immediately by a deliberate and
polite inattention. We divert our eyes from each other. Such body
language acknowledges: "I know you are there, but I would not dream
of intruding on your privacy." Sometimes an actor inadvertently
breaks through the play's illusion that permits a percipient comfortably to stare at him. That is, at the instant when eye contact is made, the
audience member is able to recognize in the person standing before
him the actual person who is performing instead of the character he is
playing. Therefore, the audience member is apt to feel the only polite
recourse is to divert his attention away from the real human being who
has caught his stare. Any worthy actor will recognize all too well
when he has "broken character." On an arena stage this can almost
never go undetected by an audience. The actor who attempts to fake
his way through a role, who provides the audience merely pretended
responses ("indicating") because he is not truly sensing those ficitonal
stimuli required to produce genuine responses will be an ineffectual
arena performer. And this is the actor whose gaze is apt to engage eye
contact with audience members precisely because it is filled by nothing which the character should be seeing.

4. Territory and body language

The techniques previously described dealt with stimuli extrin-
sic to characters in a play, but endemic stimuli is also an especially
incisive subject for expression in the arena theatres. Robert Ardrey
was probably the first artist to formally note the importance of "territoriality." It was a trait in animals which he initially observed while

working as an anthropological scientist; it suggested to him that similar instincts probably also occur in human beings. His book, *The Territorial Imperative*, presents an astounding case that such innate needs do control, or at least condition, certain human behavior.[67]

A tangible factor in shaping the space of an arena play may well result from understanding and employing territorial carving. Such carving constantly, if tacitly, affects people in their daily lives. The arena is without parallel as the most auspicious medium for expressing how such carvings condition, affect, and give nuance to human behavior, because it entails observing how space is "felt." Some obvious examples of territoriality come swiftly to mind, i.e., father's chair, mother's kitchen or sewing room, father's den or workshop, the teenager's bedroom or rumpus room.

The whole program of behavior established by territoriality and manifested through body language which is responsive to such stimuli is especially pertinent to theatre of environment. Ardrey has expressed the belief that "the territorial nature of man is genetic and ineradicable."[68] Certainly, man has a sense of territory, a need for a shell of territory around him. Julius Fast observes: "We each possess zones of territory. We carry these zones with us and we react in different ways to the breaking of these zones."[69] Observing how people guard their individual zones, (no matter how crowded the space may be where they exist, as well as how they may agress into others' zones), becomes a fascinating lesson in human behavior. These are grist for arena's mill.

Edward T. Hall has defined a new behavioral science from which he coins the term *proxemics*. What he has found can explain spatial relationships. He has elucidated what he regards as four distinct zones in which humans operate vis-a-vis other humans. The essential demarcations of these zones is correlative to the degrees of intimacy entertained between such interacting persons. He labels those four categories as : 1) intimate distance, 2) personal distance, 3) social distance, and 4) public distance. He further analyses these categories into sub-groups, namely, *close* and *far*. Clarifying the characteristics of each can provide valuable details for articulating arena space.

"Close-intimate Distance," that is, actual body contact, is occupied for making love, for very close friendships, for children clinging to parents or one another. Such distinctions were initially examined by Hall when he tried to explain the different implications of personal proximity among disparate cultures. Clearly, between adult male

Americans close-intimate distance connotes unacceptable, usually homosexual, behavior. In an Arab culture, however, or in many Mediterranean countries men frequently walk hand in hand without sending any such signals of homosexual affinity. Such cultural variants can be seen throughout the whole purview of *proxemics*. Adult American males concoct a whole body language ritual when circumstances crunch them into close-intimate spaces with other males. On crowded trains, elevators, cramped theatre seats, etc., they will follow rigid rules, holding themselves as aloof as possible, even to the point of discomfort, trying not to touch any part of their neighbors. If they do touch them, they either draw away, or tense their muscles in the touching area. Fast explains that these actions are signals: "I beg your pardon for intruding on your space, but the situation forces it and I will, of course, respect your privacy and let nothing intimate come of this."[70] To either relax or allow bodies to move easily against one another, or to enjoy the other's body heat could be to invite a verbal, or worse, a physical rebuff. Among both men and women, even a glance sustained for too many seconds in such close quarters is likely to be presumed "fresh" and rewarded with an insulting remark. A "far-intimate distance," from about six to eighteen inches, is the zone wherein such imminent physical contact threatens to occur. When another person transgresses one's far-intimate space, the tendency is to become clutched by anxiety over whether the intrusion will ultimately result in actual body touch, and one is highly set on the defensive, even when the advance is antici-pated or welcomed. It is natural, and perhaps a carry-over from evolution, for humans to instinctually feel protective of their person.

"Personal Distances," the second of Hall's categories, feature quite prominently in arena stage interplay, because many key emo-tional encounters in drama are likely to require this distance for realization. Again, please understand, there are both close and far personal distances. "Close-personal Distance" extends from around eighteen inches to thirty inches, or so. At this range, it is still possible to grasp and hold another's hand, although such action is not apt to be read as sexually suggestive so long as this distance is maintained. Nevertheless, Dr. Hall educes that while a wife can remain within this range to her husband, for another woman to come this close would presumably suggest she had designs on him, unless there were mitigating circumstances that explained her actions differently. Too, this is the ambiance for conversation klatches at some social gather-ings, cocktail parties for example. "Far-personal distance" represents the limit to which physical *domination* normally extends. Hall marks this as between thirty inches and four feet. One can no longer touch a partner comfortably at this range, so there is a consequent air of privacy to encounters held this distance apart. Still it is close enough to remain personal. People who meet on the street usually speak at this distance. Far-personal distance sometimes bespeaks "keeping one at arm's length."

The physical *domination* of territory is usually most apparent when in a state of flux. Seated in a chair, a person's physical domination of space may be confined to "far-intimate" or "close-personal" concentricities. But if one were suddenly to stand, that dominance instantly propels much farther, merely by one's preparation to move in some direction. *Preparations* are marvelously significant, even when they are also ambivalent. Remarking on such standing-up behavior by males in a public facility, Kelly Yeaton discerns:

> Merely to stand does not define the next action, nor its direction. And it might cause tension in the other males about. But to look in the direction of the men's room, and *then* rise, will not cause the waiter to come running over.[71]

Projecting a dominance over space becomes a curious prodigy which all actors attempt to master while studying their craft. Indeed, many great names in acting display precisely this uncanny ability to dominate completely vast areas of stage space, often to fill it so completely that it belies both their stature and their size. Sir Lawrence Olivier, for example, has established himself as an actor who can dominate an entire stage even when he is playing across from actors who are physically much larger than he. Other actors, Anthony Hopkins, Richard Burton, Rex Harrison, Sir John Guilgud, George C. Scott, Carroll O'Conner, Henry Fonda, as well as actresses, Katherine Hepburn, Tallula Bankhead, Mae West, Helen Hayes and dozens of other "superstars" of the modern theatre have also enjoyed reputations as large people, actors who have the ability to fill their space utterly, to dominate a stage and to assert themselves in that space so completely that their presence before an audience often belies their actual physical dimensions. To a great extent such domination is responsible for their status as great thespians as much as is their incredible acting ability and sense of characterization.

The third of Hall's zones is "Social Distance," which has both its close and far phases. From four to seven feet is the distance usually kept to conduct impersonal business—the "close-social" range. Businessmen keep this distance when meeting out of town clients, or vendors intent on selling their wares. The housewife keeps this distance from repairmen, delivery boys, or shop clerks. At casual social affairs this is a comfortable non-commital distance. Furthermore, it is an important distance for acting disciples to grasp because it can be a manipulative distance. A boss might utilize this distance, for instance, to dominate a seated employee, a secretary or receptionist. To the employee he ostensibly looms above and gains height and strength. Without so much as a conscious word, he reinforces a message of his superiority.

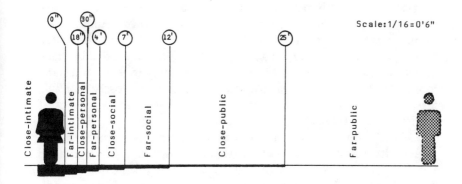

Figure 9
Zones of Inter-personal Proximity

The "far-social distance"—seven to twelve feet between subjects—affords a more formal territory for interaction; there a curious change ensues in one's ordinary eye-contact behavior. From this distance it is no longer deemed proper for people who are sustaining conversations to exchange glances briefly and then look away. Rather, it becomes mandatory to fix one another's gaze, for to do otherwise would signal excluding the opposite party from one's conversation.

At this distance the *big* boss, whose large desk deliberately creates an encumbrance between himself and his subordinates, can remain seated and still gaze at the entire figure standing before him from head to toe. This is the distance from which princely figures deal socially with their subjects. Paradoxically, married couples also often assume this far-social distance when they are at home together in the evening. It affords them the easy ambiance for conversation or reading, relaxed and under no pressure. To crowd each other into a closer proximity would impose greater urgency upon them, to one purpose or another. For the couple simply to relax in a carefree atmosphere almost surely requires that they preserve a far-social distance between them.

Finally, Hall enumerates the two sorts of "public distance." From twelve to twenty-five feet is generally the space of "near-public" transactions. One thinks of a classroom, a conference room, or a very small theatre as affording roughly near-public proximities. "Far-public" spaces, conversely, are those which exceed the twenty-five foot range. Hall considers this as typically a milieu for the public face of politicians, among other things. Certain animals in their wild state, too, will not permit humans to approach them more closely than this far-public distance. Either they will move away, themselves, or, if cornered, attack the approaching interloper.

Just studying the concept of zones which men employ to deal with each other should help arena artists bestow greater awareness of the shapes of "felt" space. In regard to this, however, one must clearly understand that cultural variants may introduce entirely new conditions upon behavior triggered by proximities. For instance, Americans generally treat space differently than people from elsewhere. Comprehending these differences can be essential, if not simply to portray characters from those other countries accurately, then at least to expand our very vision of space, itself. One such distinction in particular, noted by Hall, is how Japanese people hold a fundamentally different notion of space from Western peoples, a view that might very well contribute to arena theatre's having been so frequently misappreciated until now. Hall explains that Westerners see space as the distance between two objects. To them, space is empty. Meanwhile, the Japanese think of space, through its shape and arrangement, as having tangible meaning. They make this apparent not only in flower arrangements and art, but even in their gardens where units of space blend harmoniously to form an integrated whole.[72] That mentality which the Japanese bring to conceiving space is, in a manner of speaking, what arena can also be infusing into our (Western people's) very awareness. Arena could potentially be enlightening us about the way space conditions us.

Behavior adopted in people's quest for *privacy* will likewise be notably different in various parts of the world. These traits illustrate how varied can be the symbolic meanings of territoriality. For instance, the Japanese would have no word for privacy in their language. Crowding together in public places is not regarded as unpleasant to the Japanese, although in their homes they insist that privacy prevails. They resent intrusions into that area. Arabs, on the other hand, like to touch companions, to be able to feel and smell them. Not sharing one's breath is regarded as being ashamed. Arabs maintain no concept of privacy in public places, and think it is entirely proper, if they can do so, to push their way into lines. If Arabs need to be alone, they simple become quiet or pensive, but they do not withdraw from their fellow-beings. Americans are apt to regard such behavior as deliberate shunning and to take it as an insult. German people tend to close themselves off to gain privacy. They retreat into rooms alone and close doors to be left by themselves. Americans are not generally so rigid about closing doors, but will merely get themselves apart from other people to find privacy. The British, unlike Germans or Americans, are not apt to think of their own room as a private world. British people, possibly because of their class-conscious regimentation and also their early "nursery" room up-bringing, are left to fend for privacy only in self-withdrawal. Such contrasts in behavior could be studied across the globe and valuable insights gained by those in theatre whose job is finally to construct and articulate "images of human feeling."

A spatial structure tends to be shaped by the human life and interplay which it contains and facilitates. It should readily trigger processes which are inherent in its form. Kitchens invite and facilitate cooking; bedrooms suggest and facilitate sleeping or sexual intimacy. Considering territorial factors as well, each potential shape of an arena theatre's stage may be devised to contain similar internal cues and invitations. What, then, is the "meaning" and invitation of the *furniture*? Or the *hand-props*, such as a certain book? a statuette? telephone? writing-paper? cushions? the frying-pan? a cash register, maybe? or whatever curious incidentals could symbolically facilitate the shape of the arena space? These are the applications which territoriality so abundantly endows on the arena medium.

Body language as universal theatre

Body language, by definition, is *always* theatre. Human beings continuously exhibit body language; in its fullest sense, that is what being alive means. Shakespeare, of course, proposed that "all the world's a stage." Aside from the spectrum of human behavior from which dramatic art selects hues for its compositions, however, there is a more finite sense of the term, in which aspects of behavior—personal attitudes and body signals—convey profound non-verbal information. In that particular sector the arena finds a power which is especially fortuitous.

Unfortunately, "body language" has become a buzzword in the cant of modern society. Even theatre has not entirely avoided such pharisaism. Worse yet, today's popular obsession with body language has fostered new cottage industries dedicated to teaching the public how to favorably deport themselves before job interviewers. In other words, people are being trained to lie with a straight face. Some irreverently label this as "acting." The promise of body language centers upon how it affords communication at another level than vocalization, not that such communication is fully predictable any more than vocal language is itself ever quite precise. Among the various ways to communicate, body language may prove itself more poetical, even, than oral language. The old adage, "actions speak louder than words," does not simply mean that actions necessarily *belie* words (though sometimes they do). Rather, it indicates that motion can be the most eloquent and winning language of all.

Body language in the theatre is often perceived as an alternate vehicle for expression, alternate, of course, to oral language, which is still widely regarded as theatre's primary transmitter. Actually, that fragmentation of expressive mechanisms promulgates a myth. If one fully rationalizes the matter, spoken language certainly ought to be considered as body language, too. A *Coup de maitre* by theatre theorist Roy Mitchell, supports this very point. He expatiates about the actor's spirit of life, or what the Greeks labeled *pneuma*. This, he describes as a swirl of force within the actor of which he [the actor] is conscious and may be strongest when he is physically motionless."[73] Mitchell portrays such a force as a kind of invisible motion—

> . . . the goingness of a vital current inside the actor, which
> would manifest as visible motion if it is not restrained. It
> is more nearly what we call magnetism, less as a lodestone
> is magnetic as drawing things to it—but as a swirl is mag-

netic as sweeping things into the current it creates . . . a
vortex . . . which is the generator of all visible motion.[74]

Mitchell further suggests that it is *single*—that an actor can put this
current of impending motion, this vortex, into a gesture, *or* into his
speech, but not into both at the same instant. The audience will center
its attention only upon the element that the actor invests with this
pneuma (spirit), which the Greeks named for "the breath." Hence, the
very same "spirit of life" which might erupt as motion in the actor,
could, likewise, erupt as speech. Both are mere manifestations of only
one single spirit.

Generally, people referring to body language merely confine
their consideration to gestures or subtle postures which people sometimes strike. Those broader implications of body language which also
encompass speech usually go unrecognized. Concerning body language of the theatre, even skilled authors like Julius Fast sometimes
draw overly-narrow conclusions. Implicit, for example, in his statements concerning the theatre is the faulty fundamental notion that an
actor's task is somehow to "lie" convincingly to an audience.[75] Fast
claims that mannered, highly stylized gestures, which might be acceptable to audiences in huge theatres, will just not work when the
audience is seated close-in. This assumption is only superficially
valid. Were Fast referring simply to the sort of mimesis commonly
employed in silent films his point might seem credible. Nowadays,
though, skilled actors shift easily among media, from very large
theatres to film close-ups. They quickly realize that phoney, "indi-
cated" gestures are no more acceptable on a grand scale than in a "tight
one shot," unless, of course, these are meant to parody an action. What
Mr. Fast catalogues as an actor's "symbolic," "stylized," "rigid," or
"mannered" affectations, necessarily played large for massive theatre
audiences, are not, as he characterizes, empty, melodramatic poses
(ideograms). In large theatres gestures must spring from a source of
inner truth, quite as much as the expanding pupil of an eye should, for
a cinematic close-up. The actor simply adjusts for the magnitude of his
response. All gesture, all body language, *is* a response to the actor's
imagery. For any actor to contend otherwise would certainly result in
the worst sort of "faking," or, to use Fast's notion, lying. Even in the
ultimate Meyerhold sense, where movements are stylistically orches-
trated to effect a theatrical, choric point, they still have to emanate
from the actors' images. During his famous production of *The Govern-
ment Inspector*, Meyerhold styled a scene where eleven officials stood

"The Caretaker," by Harold Pinter, Kalamazoo [Michigan] Civic Players

"Jeepers Creepers, Here's Harry," Theatre Three, Dallas, Texas

in eleven doorways, and each simultaneously, with identical gestures, held out little packages to bribe Khelestakov. Even those mechanical, clockwork-doll characters had to generate their movements from imagery which they interiorized in order to make the action work. Mannered, stylized acting, of whatever ilk, can be equally as delicious at close-range (such as arena stages) as it ever is in large theatres. Proper imagery is what impels it to work at whatever distance.

Arenas are the theatres which seem to offer *superior* circumstances for articulating and observing body language. To be sure, film and television are often touted as media which can virtually peer down someone's nostrils, so to speak. Their great boast is in capturing galvanic reflexes which, in ordinary life, would elude casual onlookers—and magnifying these on a screen for dramatic impact. Close-up shots, replete with voice-overs on the sound track, revealing what the characters purportedly are thinking to themselves are cinema's common technique for exposition of character psychology. But, in essence, this dramatic convention is as artificial as the old"aside" technique of yesteryear, and worth no more. Although close-ups appear to give viewers great intimacy with the subject, no technique among any of the arts is more contrived. Such close-ups do not translate to behavior recognizable in every-day life. People do not ordinarily walk up to other people's faces and peer right into their eyeballs in an effort to imagine what they are thinking. Such close-ups expect the credulousness of fairytales. Neither does any repositioning of a camera to film subjects from any or all angles obviate for one second the sterile fact that photography expresses, most fundamentally, the philosophy of "scene." Film innovators constantly exhibit an odd compulsion to outwit this stolid two-dimensionality. They have even tried to run circles around their subject, cameras blazing away. No matter, for all their pains, they still end up communicating in an immutable two-dimensional language.

Arena theatre, on the other hand, affords viewers a semblance of body language in a milieu of round space. This is how its viewers would present themselves in the every-day world. Body language which they are able to observe within this medium, influenced as it is by concentric forces bearing in upon the subject from all directions, is like the body language they must themselves negotiate and react to in their own daily circumstances. Here they can discover truths of "felt" life, even emanating from highly stylized movements, which in other media would be less actualized or perhaps altogether impossible to perceive.

For ages, in one way or another, theatre has been universally portraying the images of body language. Only relatively recently has science validated the theatre's insights. A. E. Scheflen, professor of psychiatry at Albert Einstein College of Medicine, studying postures and personal "presentations," has maintained that different positions are related to different emotional states. Often these emotional states can be recaptured if a person merely resumes the original position in which they occurred. His findings grew out of the earlier James-Laing theory, which purports that emotions tend to follow actions. Theatre people, of course, have been asserting precisely these principles for generations. Michael Chekhov espoused them for actor training at least since the 1930's. More recently, Robert Benedetti wrote: "If we adopt the external or physical symptoms of an emotion, the internal fullness of that emotion will grow within us."[76]

In the nineteenth century Francois Delsarte made exhaustive inquiry into the exact physical mechanics for replicating all the various emotional states. Meyerhold's bio-mechanics, Copeau, Barrault, Artaud, Grotowski, and many others, have all, in fact if not in name, built the entire scope of their work around notions of body language. Oddly, Dr. Scheflen's very syntax of body language, including its "units," "points," "positions," and "presentations," resembles in many ways Delsarte's analytical system, devised to train actors. Now that science accepts many of these body-language insights, the public is awash in the fallout. The renowned Esalen Institute popularized encounter groups based upon body language as the principal catalyst for unblocking people's repressed emotions. Their therapies paid solemn heed to commonplace expressions of behavior. A student of theatre would instantly recognize such expressions as clichés of literature and drama: shoulder a burden; face up; chin up; grit your teeth; a stiff upper lip, bare the teeth; catch an eye; shrug it off; and so on. Each term expresses an emotion as well as a body act that signals the emotion. Such therapy was based on the notion that bodies tend to harden into set "personality-led" patterns—unhappiness revealing one form of posture, aggressiveness another, and so on. Other psychiatrists have even tied various neuroses to posture: swayed backs signal weak egos; straights backs signal inflexibility. Retracted shoulders represent repressed anger; raised shoulders impute fear; square shoulders speak of shouldering responsibility; bowed shoulders of carrying a burden. The literary origins of such observations make them no less valid. It merely indicates that artists, particularly those of the theatre, have been intuitively cognizant of such tenets long before science hailed their importance.

Since solid evidence indicates body language is already being successfully depicted in "scene" theatres, what advantage for helping man comprehend his human condition does arena offer? It is a fact the public already perceives the appearances of body language. Surely everyone recognizes stooped shoulders, or locked, resistant behavior, where arms and legs are firmly crossed. People know, more or less consciously, what the manifold signals of body language look like. However, such signals also penetrate, shape, and ordain space—that is to say, the sort of space in which people conduct their daily lives. Portraying what body language looks like is already superfluous, and unenlightening. Arena, however, becomes a school where people gain images which can help them confirm, understand, verify and appreciate what such language truly "feels" like. "School" is not intended here in the academic sense, but in the mode Langer adopts when she professes:

> Art is a public possession, because the formulation of "felt life" is the heart of any culture, and molds the objective world for people. It is their *school* [italics added] of feeling, and their defense against outer and inner chaos. It is only when nature is organized in imagination along lines congruent with forms of feeling that we can understand it, i.e., find it rational.[77]

To paraphrase an expression attributed earlier to Adolph Appia, one might say, "arena is not creating the illusion of a man with stooped shoulders, but the illusion of man in the atmosphere pervaded by his stooped shoulders." Under the figurative microscope of the arena laboratory many profound insights about the environmental effects of body language remain to be discovered. The intuition of arena artists should lead the vanguard toward such new awareness.

What seems especially perplexing is that right at this moment when such important discoveries are within reach, theatre artists largely bypass the arena medium and select other types of theatre instead. Yes, arena is politely acknowledged. Yet arena often languishes from "benign neglect." This is often done to the echoes of supercilious remarks like "it [arena] is a valid and useful staging alternative in the contemporary theatre landscape." Statistical evidence would encourage no conclusion that artists truly endorse—or even really conceive of—arena's "usefulness." Shallow lipservice, paid even by those holding long-standing arena credentials, does not constitute a "thriving arena movement." On the contrary, one is more prone to encounter assessments like the following by Cohen and Harrop: "Few ... arena stages have outlasted their novelty ... and the arena form has not reached the widespread potential its adherents anticipated."[78] Even that bastion of the true faith, Washington's formidable "Arena Stage," chose to forsake its birthright, to build a second and third *non*-arena theatre. Irrespective of such tepid acceptance, the arena medium holds out to theatre artists the most puissant means they could find to explore and articulate the human condition—to provide man images of himself in his "felt" environment. Some will clamor that "environments" are nothing new, and, indeed, *are* being created all the time by serious and avant-garde theatres the world-over. Others will protest that, after all, how they treat space in "scene" theatres (for example, on "thrust" stages), amounts to the same *as if* they were really using round space. Neither of these constituencies appreciates the one sublime factor: the crucial *completely* encircling audiences, a democracy of witnesses, a full tribunal of public discernment, ultimately compounds the magnetism on an arena stage, as on *no* other. Indeed the audience becomes like the coil wrapped around electro-magnets, potentiating the force-field. Therefore, these viewers *confirm* an arena performance—almost, one might say, as a public sacrament—and they influence the rendering of that performance in magnetic waves of assent. The radiance of those assenting impulses flowing in and out of the action in *full* circumference is an experience whose like is simply non-reproducible. Arena *is* the theatre of modern, democractic man.

The true aesthetic nature of arena theatre lies in the discovery of a simple, though profound idea: arena is the *only theatre medium* which can create motion from any degree on the compass; that is, from four opposite, decisive, intersecting polar directions *without altering* the status of audience-actor relationship.

That key aesthetic root principle, taken in conjunction with the various articulating concepts—the interplay of forces, the symbolic armature, fulfilling the play's universe, territoriality, and body language—serve to transform the arena's empty volume of space into the illusory "world" of the drama, and make this world visible through motion. The symbolic form which orients such motion "coincides unmistakably with forms of living and feeling . . . "[79] and should ultimately evoke sympathetic insight into the idea of the dramatic poem.

Notes

[1]Susanne K. Langer, *Feeling and Form* (New York: Charles Scribner's, 1953), p. 40.

[2] Langer, p. 26.

[3] Langer, p. 22.

[4] Langer, p. 26.

[5] Langer, p. 40.

[6]John Gassner, *The Theater In Our Times* (New York: Crown, 1954), p. 518.

[7] Langer, p. 46.

[8]Theodore Shank, *The Art of Dramatic Art* (New York: Dell, 1969), p. 182.

[9]Joseph Golden, *The Position and Character of Theater in the Round in the United States* (Ann Arbor: University Microfilms, Doctoral dissertation, University of Illinois, 1956), p. 59.

[10] Golden, p. 60.

[11] Golden, p. 59.

[12] Golden, p. 64.

[13] Langer, p. 47.

[14] Langer, p. 47.

[15] Langer, p. 45.

[16] Langer, p. 48.

[17] Langer, p. 68.

[18] Shank, p. 20.

[19] Shank, p. 21.

[20]Theodore M. Greene, *The Arts and the Art of Criticism* (Princeton: Princeton University Press, 1940), p. 39.

[21] Greene, p. 39.

[22] John Mason Brown, "In the Round," *Saturday Review of Literature.* April 3, 1948, p. 24-5.

[23]Richard Southern, *Open Stage* (London: Faber and Faber, 1953), p. 35.

[24] Southern, p. 13-14.

[25] Southern, p. 39-40.

[26]Note Introduction, page 6; NB also figs. 2 through 5 in chapter entitled "A Critical Reexamination."

[27]Southern, p. 39.

[28] Langer, p. 86.

[29] Adolph Hildebrand, *The Problem of Form in Painting and Sculpture* (New York: G. E. Stechert & Co., 1932).

[30] Langer, p. 87.

[31] Langer, p. 87.

[32] Langer, p. 88.

[33] Langer, p. 88.

[34] Langer, p. 89.

[35] Shank, p. 123.

[36] Langer, p. 89.

[37] Langer, p. 89-90.

[38] Langer, p. 90.

[39] Langer, p. 92.

[40] Gassner, p. 519.

[41] Stephen Joseph, *Theater in the Round* (New York: Taplinger Publishing Company, 1967), p. 17.

[42] Langer, p. 147.

[43] Langer, p. 175.

[44] Langer, p. 176.

[45] Langer, p. 184.

[46] Langer, p. 199.

[47] Augusto Boal, *Theater of the Oppressed* (New York: Urizen Books, 1979), p. 119.

[48] Langer, p. 322.

[49] Arthur Hopkins, *Reference Point* (New York: Samuel French, 1948), p. 68-9.

[50] Martin Esslin, *An Anatomy of Drama* (New York: Hill and Wang, 1979), p. 23.

[51] Shank, p. 178.

[52] Langer, p. 68.

[53] Langer, p. 325.

[54] Langer, p. 322.

[55] Eric R. Bentley, "The Drama at Ebb," *Kenyon Review*, Spring, 1945, p. 169-84.

[56] Kelly Yeaton, "Sound in the Round," (Unpublished manuscript, Pennsylvania State University, 1952). Permission to quote granted by the author.

[57] Toby Cole and Helen K. Chinoy, *Directors On Directing* (New York: Bobbs-Merrill, 1963), p. 42.

[58] Kelly Yeaton, "Arena Staging," *Producing The Play*. Ed. John Gassner (New York: Dryden Press, 1953, p. 572.

[59] Arthur Michel, "The Modern Dance in Germany," *Modern Dance*. Ed. Merle Armitage (New York: E. Weyhe, 1953), p. 5).

[60] Langer, p. 324.

[61] Suzanne K. Langer, *Philosophy In A New Key* (New York: Mentor Books, 1948), p. 231.

[62] Langer, *New Key*, p. 231-2.

[63] John Millington Synge, *The Complete Plays of J. M. Synge* (New York: Vintage Books, Random House, 1960), p. 119-73.

[64] Julius Fast, *Body Language* (New York: Pocket Books, 1970), p. 129.

[65] Fast, p. 129.

[66] Fast, p. 130.

[67] Robert Ardrey, *The Territorial Imperative* (New York: Atheneum, 1966).

[68] Fast, p. 15.

[69] Fast, p. 17.

[70] Fast, p. 21.

[71] Based on personal correspondence between Kelly Yeaton and the writer, April 22, 1984. Permission to quote granted by Yeaton.

[72] Fast, p. 28.

[73] Roy Mitchell, *Creative Theater* (New York: John Day, 1929), p. 187.

[74] Mitchell, p. 188.

[75] Fast, p. 26-7.

[76] Robert L. Benedetti, *The Actor at Work: An Introduction to the Skills of Acting* (Englewood Cliffs, NJ: Prentice-Hall, Inc., 1970), p. 43.

[77] Langer, *Feeling*, p. 409.

[78] Robert Cohen and John Harrop, *Creative Play Direction* (Englewood Cliffs, NJ: Prentice-Hall, Inc., 1970), p. 56.

[79] Langer, *Feeling*, p. 68.

SPECIFYING THE CASE FOR ARENA THEATRE
AND WHAT IT MEANS

Thus far, no plays have been written exclusively for arena performance. The opportunity to create works geared only for arenas has hitherto been disregarded by talented playwrights. Such scripts would explicitly articulate concepts of feeling that could only be achieved with round space. Meanwhile, arenas have had no choice but to make-do with plays originally written for "scene theatres," which forces them to operate in a sort of time-warp. At present, most playwrights are unlikely candidates to rush into this breach. The economics of theatre afford them little incentive to create for insubstantial markets, and the number of arena theatres remains small.

When any scripts have, in the past, achieved artistic fulfillment via arena productions, they were bold products of valid reconceptualizations; but even works that have best succeeded in arenas were never originally written for the round. Some few insightful directors, dedicated to creating genuine art-works employing the arena medium, set about their chores by first carefully analyzing what plays to produce. Such analyses probed far beyond determining merely whether a play's action depended heavily upon using actual doors or windows, or entailed stairs, trap-doors, or other practical scenic devices. From the very first, these directors formulate such works in environmental, not scenic, symbols. They realize they are dealing with a different symbolic language. Although such directorial conceptualizations probably do not parallel visual images of the work ("opposite the eye, and related directly and essentially to the eye"), as concocted by the playwright, they nonetheless carefully serve the spirit which the playwright evokes. That spirit must be capable of *unequivocal enhancement* through the inherent qualities of round space. Directors today are seldom trained to "think" in terms of round-space symbols. Often one finds inappropriate plays being skewered into the round in blatant disregard for either the play's or an arena's inherent qualities.

The presumption that any script can be adapted to an arena

format can often lead to disastrous theatrical results. Like many other directors, I previously believed that any show whatsoever could become viable for an in-the-round presentation regardless of what theatre method was first conceived for it. I believed that minor changes in scenic conventions would be necessary, and I also believed that these could be accomplished without violating the spirit of the playwright's work.

A few years ago, in response to a challenge to test my theory put forth by Marston Balch, director of Tufts Arena Theatre, I undertook to stage a production of Anton Chekhov's *The Three Sisters*. Balch's idea was to see how the Russian playwright's conception of contrapuntal dialogue—that is, dialogue that comments upon the major action of the play but emanating from background characters absorbed in their own detached activities and uninvolved in the principal action—could be handled in a round format.

Chekhov's original use of this technique seems to have been construed heretofore and in traditional proscenium staging to allow the characters to "upstage" the principals when they made their ironic and often humorous commentary. (Obviously, in film, the technique of "cross-cutting" would diminish the "upstaging" by featuring the two scenes as taking place at the same time by means of careful editing.) But such asides are crucial to articulate the spirit of what was really occurring in the play; hence, two points of focus are created, one acting as a subsidiary for the other, both occurring simultaneously. As an example, Colonel Vershinin, a married army officer and Masha, the daughter and hostess of the household where the play is set, engage one another in a symbolic scene that reflects on their unfulfilled passion while in the house's sitting room. Others, including Masha's brother and some officers, who are involved at a card table in a nearby room, continue to play and talk throughout the scene; their voices occasionally grow loud enough for certain snatches of dialogue to be heard clearly. The card table conversation is completely detached from the scene between Colonel Vershinin and Masha; however, in counterpoint, it intones a mocking and cynical comment on the difficulties involving the Colonel and his frustrated young companion. On the face of things, the staging problem seems easy to solve; it merely requires double, simultaneous centers of action, one of which will be subordinate to the other.

Arena theatre, however, cannot subordinate focus through perspective. To an encircling audience, one person's foreground becomes someone else's background. By use of elevation and lighting effects, however, one can accentuate one scene or another at different times or at the same time. Thus, by dividing the stage and elevating the sitting room by means of a six-inch platform, the two-room effect was created. By down-lighting the card room, a further reduction of emphasis on the playing group was achieved, and this effect was enhanced by minimizing the mime and dumb-show of the card game. By substituting such conventions and utilizing other theatrical methods, I was able to create the dual focus and to articulate the points of the play while working it in an arena format.

Unfortunately, in spite of the physical success of overcoming the staging difficulties, I ultimately realized that *The Three Sisters* was not a suitable play for arena production, not because the impediments to an in-the-round staging could not be managed, but because the symbolic theme of Chekhov's script is directly at odds with the philosophical nature of arena expression.

My production made the same mistake directors have made when they have failed to understand what it means to think in terms of round-space symbols. It is not sufficient merely to address what has to be done to accomplish the staging of a play in an arena medium; more crucially, one must analyze *why* the play should be performed in arena in the first place. At bottom, the problem is whether or not the aesthetic faculties of arena theatre speak to the substance of the play. If such a staging enhances and articulates the work, then such a staging format is not only suitable, it very well may be necessary to display the work in its best environment, its best space. But if the arena simply affords an alternate route for navigating the work into per-formance, then the director has betrayed not only a playwright's script, he also has betrayed the underlying philosophy of arena staging itself.

Writing about the *Inspector General*, Jan Kott calls attention to an unusual emphasis on eating in Gogol's script. Kott conveys an observation by Levi-Strauss that "the perspective of our traditional culture ... likes to contrast the pathos of unhappy love and the comedy of a full stomach." Kott concludes the statement with a comment of his own: "In Gogol food is also riddled with rank and place."[1] The same statement could be applied to *The Three Sisters*. Kott declared Gogol to be the initiator of a new genre: "tragic farce," something that also might be equally applied to Chekhov. Remarking on this genre, Kott states: "The end of one comedy creates the beginning of the next one. All roles are cast forever." This supports his further discussion where he speaks of "enforced roles—the terrible and the preordained roles—

that are foisted upon each of us by family, authority, property, gender, youth or old age."[2]

Life perceived in such relentless, bleak terms as these is *a priori* hierarchical, and anti-heroic. *The Three Sisters* seems emblematic of the conflict between symbolic theme and environmental expression; the sisters' desire to move "to Moscow ... to Moscow" seems to emphasize the atmospheric center of the theme and, not incidentally, to lend the play's mode to the arena technique because of the obvious emphasis on space and a transmigration of locale—rural to urban, for instance. But what might be mistaken as an environmentally based theme is actually expressive of an hierarchical and anti-heroic outlook that is clear through the play's imagery: For the Serghyeevna sisters, "Moscow" actually represents nothing more than a place where they may fulfill preordained roles. They rank themselves as proper ladies in dignified society and cling to delusions of themselves as ladies in a rural town and imagine that a fashionable life awaits them in the big city. They neither manipulate their own destinies, nor do they attempt to do so. They are not pioneers, searchers, free spirits, something that is essential to plays appropriate for arena theatres. In no way do these Chekhovian characters anticipate creating a "new" environment through their desire for relocation; rather, they want their present environment—their *status quo*—transplanted to an atmosphere which they imagine is more suited to their rank, their place in society. They are not initiators of new directions, searchers for new environments, but victims, hierarchical parasites.

Hierarchies are linear, two-dimensional, planar apparitions. They require man to accede to a cosmology based upon a "principle of perspective" which defines man's consciousness of order in the universe. Social man assigns classes, ranks, and other criteria to measure an individual's place in the human schema; indeed, the public's very mode of cognition as well as the scope of its imagination is delimited and constricted by terms accessible through the symbolic vocabulary of hierarchies. Even in a democratic society where ranks and orders are established by other means than birth or power, society seems adamant that every individual—particularly every individual on stage—be classified according to an hierarchical, two-dimensional plan that permits linear movement, but rarely allows for three dimensional change.

Hierarchies do not liberate or empower man; on the contrary, they deny him his unique capacity to create and negotiate his way through life. In arena theatre, space which is inherently linear and planar does *not* exist; rather, matrix-like and synergistic space permits negotiations of power to be transacted in three-dimensional, life-and-death terms. Thus, producing a play which symbolically evokes inertial hierarchies for the arena theatre ultimately cannot help but combat the aesthetic faculties inherent to the arena medium. The result is a detriment to both the play and the circular mode of theatre in which it is expressed.

A different aspect of the problem is revealed in another example found in a production of *Painting Churches* staged by The Cassius Carter Centre Stage, part of San Diego's Old Globe performing arts complex. The play was in no way enhanced by the arena format. Rather than augmenting the articulation of the playwright's point for the audience, the arena medium fought the script's message all the way through. Indeed, the decision to use a round format for the production seemed accidental as the title alone seems to disqualify the play for staging in arena. The theme of the piece, moreover, is antithetical to arena treatment.

The story line of the script dwells on a young woman, daughter to Mr. Gardner Church, once a famous New England poet. There is also a mother who is descended from Boston's elite society, a true Brahman. Growing up in the shadow of two such prominent parents has rendered the daughter insecure about her own worth. She develops a talent for portrait-painting to validate her identity and self-image. Moving home, ostensibly to help them relocate to smaller quarters, she wants to paint their portrait in order to exorcise her repressed childhood fears and overcome the inhibitions they have created in her, to diminish their psychological influence over her and to come to terms with her domineering parents by rendering them into "a perspective" on canvas. In fact, the principal action of one major scene involves her trying to select the correct *background* for the portrait setting—even to the extent of draping certain fabrics to embellish the *scene*. In the denoument, she presents them with a finished portrait.

A more suitable title to attempt an arena production might have been "*Sculpturing*" *Churches*, or perhaps, "*Church Sculptures*," for the director abused the arena form and kinetic space throughout. To accomplish the actions of the play, many set items, actors, and even the action of the play itself spilled out into the aisles. The skeletal frame of some windows (ultimately employed as the "scene" for the portrait setting) blocked off one aisle entirely, thus attempting to set up a presentational axis in a medium which, by nature, can't have one.

This production demonstrated today's synthetic literacy concerning the arena medium, something that is particularly disturbing as the Cassius Carter Centre Stage is one of the few remaining professional arena theatres operating in the country. Yet such astounding dissonance with the viabilities of arena staging are almost as common anywhere arena theatres continue to function.

In Houston's Alley Theatre, for example, a permanent arena format is used for an entire season, and the criteria for selecting plays for staging in this small basement auditorium seems to be based more on audience drawing potential for a given play than upon any specific philosophical or thematic method of selection. Simply put, the upstairs proscenium theatre seats more people, so the less *avant garde*, more traditional scripts are staged there, while those with more limited appeal or the potential for smaller and more intimate audiences are relegated to the basement. No systematic judgement seems to guard against plays which are entirely unsuitable for a circular format being staged there, and in recent seasons everything from *The Gin Game* to *Cloud Nine* have been shoehorned into arena staging regardless of their themes. The rule seems to be that if a director can overcome the physical and technical difficulties of mounting a play in an arena theatre, then it is fine to do so.

Houston's Alley, however, is just one of many houses in the country where an arena theatre was constructed with specific theatrical opportunities in mind but which is now used much as any other auditorium might be used. Whatever artistic intention was imagined when these facilities were built has been forgotten, and arena staging simply means alternative staging, usually for smaller houses and riskier box office potential.

Not even television is immune from such a misuse of the arena format. The obvious problem of trying to "round out" a medium which is by definition two-dimensional may be put aside as one considers the difficulties of a stand-up comic trying to joke into a camera lens while simultaneously attempting to "work" his live arena audience. A comedian's stock in trade is facial expression—pans, takes, double-takes, false asides, etc.—and if half or more of an audience is behind him, his ability to enhance his verbal expression is not only hampered, it likely is deadened as those to his rear try to figure out by watching the faces of their opposite numbers in the audience facing him what he is doing with his gestures. Arena staging for comedy of this sort—or much comedy of any sort—can be crippling.

Perhaps even more unusual is the attempt to stage such productions as *A Chorus Line* in arena theatre. Carried to a logical conclusion, playing a musical song-and-dance show such as this one in-the-round would seem to underscore the antithesis of the idea behind arena theatre. This particular play seems to convey a metaphor about the flat, linear condition of the lives of its characters, and by implication of all life generally. The diametrical opposite is connoted in the meaning of arena staging. Surely such inappropriate selections are as detrimental to the scripts as they are abusive to the form of arena theatre.

A virtual litany of arena theatre mismatches could continue, for abuses caused by forcing unsuitable plays into a round format increase as more and more arena stages are turned over to amateurs and semi-professional groups who have no awareness of the enormously significant philosophical implications of using the round form. But the point should be clear: arena staging is suited only to specific plays whose theme and message are best articulated with a round stage encircled by an audience. The script at hand should be selected precisely for its suitability to the form of production; to force a script into one form or another for non-artistic reasons denies the integrity of both the playwright's work and the theatre artist's attempt to interpret it.

As reason for their day-to-day existence, theatres-in-the-round have thus far been unprepared to offer a systematic exposition of the theoretical basis of their work. Before such an offering can take place, however, theatre artists must come to understand what an arena theatre is, what it *means* to stage a play in one, and what differences, not only in the boundaries, but in the *significance* of staging potential, exist in the round format. The point is not to restrict use of arena theatre, but to expand its cultural influence through its proper use. Artists must actively seek out, or create themselves, appropriate works for arena theatre.

Artists who employ arena staging must demonstrate their complete understanding of the relationship of "round space" to "scene" and, as well, their cognizance of the relationship of those concepts to the thematic content of a given play. If art is supposed to be "the creation of forms symbolic of human feelings," then clearly, arena theatre's indigenous form must proceed to articulate such feelings. Otherwise, as the German philosopher, Hegel, states: "the work of art [will be] a thing divided against itself, in which form and content no longer appear as grown into one."[3] A play's contents may demonstrate one concept of human feeling, while its form—its staging—eventually distracts by articulating quite another. The arena theatre, due to its very form, imparts a *libertarian* expression of the human condition—a struggle for freedom from constricting, two-dimensional hierarchies which belong to the procrustean outlook of earlier ages—reflected in other forms or modes of staging. The fundamental spirit of arena staging is pioneering, competitive, expansive, assertive, positive, ebullient. It is, itself, a struggle for freedom of expression, and the implications of this concept are far-reaching.

Arena theatres crave the kinds of drama and sorts of events which emphasize character, moods and images expressing this struggle for liberation, for freedom unrestricted by a two-dimensional, non-linear, non-planar existence, and everything that implies. Arena is not merely some sort of pollyanna-theatre; nor is it merely a disorganized circle of empty space which offers a different set of challenges to a director. It also is not a theatre of alienation. Instead of all of these, arena's coherent, natural *raison d'être* is to convey a libertarian view of the human condition, a condition that yearns to achieve freedom of the human spirit and a desire for unencumbered, unrestricted, non-hierarchical human existence. Within such a guideline, there is enormous scope for exploration. But the important question is not "How to do it?" Rather, it is "Why to do it?" The essential task of answering this belongs to the theatre artists themselves: the directors, the actors, and, most certainly, the writers. They must consolidate their artistic visions to create unique works of arena art, and continually look forward to the day when theatre artists everywhere will find in the arena theatre their most congenial medium for modern expression.

The case and coherent meaning of arena theatre may, then, be found in understanding it as a metaphor for the modern zeitgeist. Arena is truly a precious vessel for our cultural patrimony. From its locus one discovers an entirely different sort of cosmology, a new way to understand nature and our lives. Arena offers new dramatic insights to cement and strengthen our shared bond of human experience. Whereas "scene theatres," in the metaphoric sense, create images of a social hierarchy (by definition an outmoded concept of the human condition)—arena theatres create images which bespeak the workings of the "level playing field." Arena's symbolic vocabulary of round space imparts a modern, relevant concept of the human condition. The manifesto for arena is not absorbed with "putting on shows" (affectations). Rather, it is concerned with man doing deeds of courage, conviction, and will power. Popular western writer Louis L'Amour remarked during the last years of his life: "In three generations space will be our new conquest of the West, our new American Dream." The hallmark or emblem of arena theatre might be characterized as somewhat like a pursuit of that dream. In a very real sense, it is about man's voyage, his quest into unknown space, his conquest of new frontiers, his futurist adventure; and, significantly, this adventure, this dream, is no more restricted to Americans than is the meaning behind the world's drama. Perhaps more than any other genre, the drama is the least parochial; for within the confines of *the play*, man so often finds his deepest fears and his greatest joys, his darkest evils and his brightest humors displayed in a cathartic, vicarious, and illuminating brilliance that often touches his very soul and brings forth those two most definitive of human capabilities: laughter and tears.

In a very real sense, man's need for validation, for power negotiation with nature, god, and his fellow man is as great now as it was when primitive dancers moved about their prehistoric fires and displayed the commonplace tragedies and comedies learned from their own experience. As the modern world ventures into new negotiations of powers, the self-creation and self-definition of individuals necessary to meet and overcome challenges of the future are precisely the images by which arena theatre instructs mankind. Negation, pessimism, fear and destruction, habiliments of the old-world order, are supplanted by the Westering ideals of this unique medium: building, improving, edifying. This is the essence of the meaning of theatre; this is the essence of the meaning of drama. Now drama, exhibited through the unique symbolic vocabulary of arena theatre, freshly and vibrantly asserts the vital truth and intrinsic value behind the idea that the proper redemption of man (both in religious and secular contexts) begins with knowing himself.

Notes

[1] Jan Kott, *The Theater of Essence and Other Essays* (Evanston: Northwestern University Press, 1984), p. 13.
[2] Kott, p. 13.
[3] Bernard Bosanquet, trans., *Introduction to Hegel's Philosophy of Fine Art* (London: Kegan Paul, Trench & Co., 1886), p. 183.

BIBLIOGRAPHY

Ardrey, Robert. *The Territorial Imperative*. New York: Atheneum, 1966.

"A Sermon Against Miracle Plays." Anon. *Dramatic Theory and Criticism*. Ed. Bernard Dukore. New York: Holt, Rinehart and Winston, 1974.

Atkinson, Brooks. "Arena Theater." *New York Times*, May 1, 1949, Sec. 2, p. 1.

Benedetti, Robert L. *The Actor At Work: An Introduction to the Skills of Acting*. Englewood Cliffs, NJ: Prentice-Hall, Inc., 1970.

Bentley, Eric R. *In Search Of Theater*. New York: Crown, 1954.

—. "The Drama at Ebb." *Kenyon Review*, Spring, 1945, p. 169-84.

Boal, Augusto. *Theater of the Oppressed*. New York: Urizen Books, 1979.

Bosanquet, Bernard. trans. *Introduction to Hegel's Philosophy of Fine Arts*. London: Kegen Paul, Trench & Co., 1886.

Boyle, Walden. *Central and Flexible Staging*. Berkeley: University of California Press, 1956.

Brown, John Mason. "In the Round." *Saturday Review of Literature*. April 3, 1948, 31:24-5.

Bullough, Edward. "Psychical Distance as a Factor in Art and an Aesthetic Principle." *British Journal of Medicine*, June, 1912.

Bush, Catherine. "View From The Top, John Jesurun's Cinematic Theatre." *Theatre Crafts*, August -September, 1985.

Cohen, Robert and Harrop, John. *Creative Play Direction*. Englewood Cliffs, NJ: Prentice-Hall, Inc., 1974.

Cole, Toby and Chinoy, Helen K. *Directors On Directing*. New York: Bobbs-Merrill, 1963.

Craig, Edward Gordon. *On The Art of the Theater*. New York: Theater Arts Books, 1960.

Esslin, Martin. *An Anatomy of Drama*. New York: Hill and Wang, 1979.

Fast, Julius. *Body Language*. New York: Pocket Books, 1970.

Freud, Ralph. "Central Staging is Really Old Stuff." *Players Magazine*, December, 1948, p. 52-3.

Gassner, John. *The Theater In Our Times*. New York: Crown, 1954.

—. Personal correspondence with Mr. Grove, November, 1956.

Goffman, Erving. *Behavior in Public Places*. The Free Press, 1969.

—. *Presentation of Self in Everyday Life*. Garden City, NY: Anchor Books, 1959.

Golden, Joseph. "The Position and Character of Theater in the Round in the United States." Ph.D. dissertation, University of Illinois, 1956.

Greene, Theodore M. *The Arts and the Art of Criticism*. Princeton: Princeton University Press, 1940.

Hall, Edward T. *The Hidden Dimension*. Garden City, NY: Doubleday, 1966.

Haskell, Arnold. *The Wonderful World of Dance*. Garden City, NY: Garden City Books, 1960.

Hildebrand, Adolph. *The Problem of Form in Painting and Sculpture*. New York: G.E. Stechert & Co., 1932.

Hopkins, Arthur. *Reference Point*. New York: Samuel French, 1948.

Jones, Margo. *Theater-in-the-Round*. New York: Rinehart, 1951.

Joseph, Stephen. *Theater in the Round*. New York: Taplinger Publishing Company, 1967.

Koons, Martha Ann. "The Development of Arena Theater in America As Reflected In Periodical Literature 1940-1950." M.A. thesis, Pennsylvania State University, 1951.

Kott, Jan. *The Theater of Essence and Other Essays*. Evanston: Northwestern University Press, 1984.

Langer, Susanne K. *Feeling and Form*. New York: Charles Scribner's Sons, 1953.

—. *Philosophical Sketches*. Baltimore: The Johns Hopkins Press, 1962.

—. *Philosophy In A New Key*. New York: Mentor Books, 1948.

—. *Problems of Art*. New York: Charles Scribner's Sons, 1957.

—. *Reflections On Art*. Baltimore: The Johns Hopkins Press, 1958.

Lauterer, Arch. "Speculations on the Value of Modern Theater Forms." *NTC Bulletin*, December, 1949, 11:11-18.

Macgowan, Kenneth. "Theater in the Round." *New York Times*, March 21, 1948, Sec. 2, p. 1.

Macgowan, Kenneth and William Melnitz. *The Living Stage*. New York: Prentice Hall, 1955.

Marowtiz, Charles. *Stanislavski And The Method*. New York: Citadel Press, 1964.

Michel, Arthur. "The Modern Dance in Germany." *Modern Dance*, Ed. Merle Armitage. New York: E. Weyhe, 1953.

Mitchell, Roy. *Creative Theater*. New York: John Day, 1929.

Popkin, Henry. "The Drama Vs. the One-Ring Circus." *Theater Arts*, February, 1951, 35:39-42.

Rosenfield, John. "Dallas Theater '48." *Think*, April, 1948.

Scheflen, A. E. "Human Communications." *Behavioral Science*, Vol. 13, 1968.

Southern, Richard. *Open Stage*. London: Faber and Faber, 1953.

—. *The Medieval Theater in the Round*. New York: Theater Arts Books, 1975.

Synge, John Millington. *The Complete Plays of J. M. Synge*. New York: Vintage Books, Random House, 1960.

Villiers, André. *Le Théâtre en Rond*. Paris: Librairie Théâtrale, 1958.

Yeaton, Kelly. "Arena Staging." *Producing The Play*. Ed. John Gassner. New York: Dryden Press, 1953.

—. "Sound in the Round." Unpublished manuscript, Pennsylvania State University, 1952. [Permission granted by author.]

—. Personal Correspondence with Mr. Grove, April 22, 1984. [Permission granted by author.]

INDEX